# FLEE FROM THE PAST

# FLEE FROM
# THE PAST

## Carolyn G. Hart

**Five Star**
**Unity, Maine**

Five Star Mystery.
Published in conjunction with Tekno-Books and
Ed Gorman.

Cover photograph by Jason Johnson.

November 1998
Standard Print Hardcover Edition.

Five Star Standard Print Mystery Series.

The text of this edition is unabridged.

Set in 11 pt. Plantin by Rick Gundberg.

Printed in the United States on permanent paper.

**Library of Congress Cataloging in Publication Data**

Hart, Carolyn G.
  Flee from the past / Carolyn G. Hart.
    p.   cm.
    ISBN 0-7862-1661-1 (hc : alk. paper)
    I. Title.
  PS3558.A676F58   1998
  813´.54—dc21                                    98-42596

To Phil,
always

# I

I had lost one love six years before. I didn't intend to lose Paul. Six years ago I had cut and run because I'd had no choice, and I left love behind. I had twisted and turned and covered my tracks, driven by fear.

Six years is a long time. I had grown confident. If no one had found me, questioned me in six years, then I should be safe. I was wary, of course. I never quite relaxed the guard on my tongue. There were so many little things always to remember. No, I could never be entirely at ease, but I had truly come to feel more secure. What could threaten Dr. Hamilton's wife, Janey?

What, indeed?

Sometimes I wondered if I couldn't gamble just a little. Not much, just a little. I stood on the front porch in the chill grayness just before dawn and watched the backlights of Paul's MG disappearing around the corner and I wished that this time I had taken a chance and gone with him.

I dropped the hand that I had been waving. Paul was gone. He had been unhappy that I'd refused to go. He was too mild of temper, too even in his calm appraisal of life to be angry. Anger wasn't his response ever. But I had hurt him this time with my refusal to travel.

It was only that I felt so safe in Lancaster. It was a long, long way from Italy. I had settled into Lancaster five years ago, the young wife Dr. Hamilton brought back from his year as a visiting professor at a junior college south of Los Angeles.

At first his colleagues were a little hostile, a little distant. They and their wives, like Paul, were in their mid-thirties. Who, they wondered, was this pale girl who had married an older man and would now be the wife of the department chairman?

Slowly, with infinite care and patience, I made my place. Dr. Hamilton's wife. Janey Hamilton, Paul's wife. And later, Janey Hamilton, Margaret's mother. It had been easy, melding into place, because I was supremely happy. I loved Paul. I loved my daughter. I loved Lancaster. And it was all doubly precious because I had not expected ever to love again. I had thought, until I met Paul, that happiness was foreclosed to me.

Always, though, there was a dark edge of uncertainty to my happiness, a somber awareness of the fragility of life and love. I never forgot that I had loved once before, gloriously, passionately, and that I had been forced to run away from that love. Sometimes, happy as I was, grateful as I was to be safe and cared for in Lancaster, I would mourn that first love and wish it back. Then, swiftly, I would dismiss that thought, that desire, and be fiercely grateful for Paul and Margaret.

The past throws long shadows into the present. Now I realized that my happiness was being threatened not by my romantic memories of the past but by my fear of travel. Not, of course, that Paul would turn away from me merely because I would not travel with him. Yet it is small irritants which can begin to erode a marriage.

I stood unhappily on my front porch and stared down the street after a car long on its way to the airport. Up to now, it hadn't been difficult to avoid travel. At first there had been no push to travel since Paul was just back from a year's absence. Then my pregnancy made it easy to say, "Later, we'll do that later." Later there was a baby, and it is hard to make arrangements to leave a baby behind. But Margaret was four now and she loved our maid, Willamae. This morning Paul had said eagerly, "Let's ask Willamae to stay with Margaret and then you can come to Toronto with me. It will be fun, Janey."

I reminded him of the luncheon I was going to have on Wednesday to welcome the wives of new members of the department, and he had nodded, the eagerness seeping out of his face.

So he went without me. I watched him walk down the steps, an even paced, deliberate man, dignified and formal. He stopped at the door of his MG and looked back at me and there was almost a frown on his narrow, ascetic face. Then his mouth, a kindly generous mouth, spread in a smile. "Take care, Janey. See you next week."

He was in his car and gone.

Next time, I decided abruptly, I would go. Then I remembered that Paul had talked about a conference in Belgium. I had no passport, of course. Did I dare apply for one?

I shivered and drew my robe tighter around me, then turned and opened the big front door and stepped into the foyer. I was shutting the door when I heard the swift slap of small bare feet on the uncarpeted treads of the main stairway. Looking up, I smiled and held out my arms to the small figure flying down the steps, her soft cotton nightgown streaming out behind her. In one hand she held a fluffy orange stuffed rabbit, a limp survivor of an Easter basket. The other hand she stretched out toward me.

"Mommy, hey mommy!"

I gathered her up in my arms and pressed my face against her straggly little girl hair, then asked, "What woke you, Margaret? It's way too early for little girls to be up."

"A big blue jay and he's mad at Glady!" She was looking at

me out of huge gray eyes and her face was like a delicate miniature of her father's, deepset eyes, narrow nose, and high angular cheekbones.

She wiggled free and grabbed my hand, then led me through the living room to the door that opened onto the screened-in porch. She began to tussle with the hard-to-turn knob. I was reaching forward to help when she squared her thin shoulders and firmly shook her head. "I can do it. I can."

So I waited and she pulled and tugged and worked until she managed to open the heavy door. She stepped out onto the screened-in porch and I followed.

She pointed up at the old elm that climbed right up next to her windows. There, squalling angrily on a low branch, was a raucous blue jay. Walking daintily beneath the tree was Gray Lady, our nondescript cat.

"Glady, Glady," Margaret called as Gray Lady pawed through the dew-damp grass in the front yard. The cat paused, looked back over her gray and black striped self, stared as though she had never seen us before, then turned her face away and continued calmly on.

"Glady!" Margaret called imperiously.

I laughed. "It's no use, baby. Gray Lady knows we aren't supposed to be on the screened-in porch at this hour of the morning. I should be in the kitchen and you should be in bed. No sensible cat will deal with out-of-place people. She's on her way right now around the house to the kitchen."

Sure enough, we found Gray Lady waiting expectantly on the top step of the back porch. Margaret held open the screen door and the cat entered with sharp, friendly meows and went directly to the cupboard where her dry cereal was stored. While Margaret fed Gray Lady, I fixed breakfast for her. I had eaten early with Paul.

Margaret was half finished with her cantaloupe when she

looked up at me in sudden thought. "Where's daddy?"

"He's gone to the airport. To catch a plane to Toronto."

"Where's that?"

I tried to explain where Canada was and how long it would take the big plane to fly there.

She listened politely, then asked, "Can daddy take me to the park this afternoon?"

I smiled and shook my head. Margaret has yet to categorize her days into slots for work or play. Today was Monday, a work day for her daddy, whether here or away, and a preschool day for her. But she didn't wake and think, "Today is Monday," or "Today is Saturday." She woke and saw each day without any strictures.

"Daddy will be gone all week, honey, but I'll take you to the park this afternoon. Unless something comes up."

She nodded, satisfied.

I drank a cup of coffee while she ate her cereal and then it was time to hurry up the stairs and get ready for preschool. Every morning I felt the same odd mixture of irritation and amusement. It seemed inconceivable that such a small person with only four years of history could be so determinedly independent. Margaret knew which dress she wished to wear each day — and she would put it on by herself and button it and tie her shoes, thank you very much. The more difficult the task, the straighter the small mouth set itself. I realized that her chubby little fingers managed ably; her father's daughter.

However, I insisted that she let me help brush her hair, her flyaway little girl's hair, and smooth it back and up into a saucy ponytail with a gay little bow.

The minutes were running out; it was eight-thirty and time to leave, but we had to pause for a moment to find a show-and-tell. No, mother, not a doll! Everyone has a doll. No, it must be something to show and tell about! I urged a

11

music box, a picture book, a wooden puzzle. She shook her head and stood in the front hall, her fine light eyebrows drawn in thought.

"Margaret dear, we must hurry. You can take a show-and-tell tomorrow."

Again she shook her head, then suddenly her face lightened and she turned to run back toward the kitchen. In a moment she was back, her face full of triumph and one hand closed tight. She held it up and opened her fingers and I saw the sticky mound of cantaloupe seeds.

It was a happy morning, this Monday morning, Margaret beside me in the Mercedes, filling my morning with the joy of a child's delight in a handful of cantaloupe seeds. I drove slowly, in no hurry to speed my day, past the old-fashioned frame houses, many of them now welcoming student boarders. Two blocks, three, then the high stone wall that marked the boundaries of St. Mary's Church and School rose on my right.

Margaret wriggled eagerly in her seat. I turned into the drive and stopped at the side door used by the preschool. I reached over and unbuckled Margaret's seat belt and started to open the door, but no, she would do it by herself, and climb out and push the door shut by herself, too.

"Have a good morning, Margaret," I called after her.

She nodded and turned away, and I heard her light, happy voice as she greeted the teacher standing duty at the door. "Good morning, Mrs. Harrison," and she was inside.

I smiled as I drove home. My dauntless daughter.

The tempo of the morning began to pick up after I reached home. There were two phone calls in a row. Phoebe Blair asked me to play tennis on Wednesday and I had to say no because of the luncheon. She had no other free morning so we settled on Wednesday a week. The second caller was Mrs.

Marley, the organizer of volunteers at the Oliver Workman hospital. She wanted to know if Thursday afternoons would be agreeable to me throughout the fall instead of Tuesdays, and I said yes.

I was finishing my rather formal conversation with Mrs. Marley, one of those faint-voiced women whom you never know well, when I heard a light tap on the kitchen door, then it opened and Willamae came in. I smiled and nodded good morning, then said briskly into the receiver, "Don't worry about the change at all, Mrs. Marley. Thursdays will be fine." I listened again for a moment, then said, I hoped firmly, "I will see you on Thursday then, Mrs. Marley. It was good of you to call." I hung up the phone with a sense of escape. How difficult it was sometimes to avoid rudeness. If only people like Mrs. Marley wouldn't try to wrap you in tentacles of talk, absorbing your time, pressing to hold you for another moment, a few more words. I blew a little spurt of air in irritation. But I knew why I stood and talked, why I wasn't rude. She was a lonely old woman and the organization of volunteers gave her entrée to your home, even if only electronically. I remembered the loneliness of a very young child, surrounded by others but belonging to no one, and so I stood and talked and listened. Was I offering up little placations? Oh yes, if I were honest. And I knew their efficacy was on a par with clutching a rabbit's foot or keeping a buckeye handy. More civilized perhaps, but no more effective.

Willamae had assembled the mop and pail and cleanser by the time I turned away from the telephone. She moved quickly and efficiently. She looked up and smiled when she realized I was watching her. She was tall and trim and graceful and withdrawn. I had never felt sure of Willamae's age or, really, of anything else about her. She worked with an economy of motion. She spoke crisply when spoken to but did not initiate conversations. She had been working for me twice every week since I'd first come to Lancaster. At first her almost-regal silence intimidated me but, from the day I brought Margaret home from the hospital, I counted Willamae my friend because she welcomed Margaret too and grew to love her. We live in strained times. The old unlovely servility is gone but two women in a house cannot comfortably be employer and employee unless there is either formality or friendship. Our relationship was an odd mixture of the two. I hesitated to presume a friendship though I often felt that Willamae liked me.

"Good morning, Willamae."

"Good morning, Mrs. Hamilton."

For an instant I felt that old sense of discomfort. Why shouldn't I call her Mrs. Childers? But no, that would be wrong too, making a point of it.

"Before you start on the floors, Willamae, let's check my plans for the luncheon. Do you think two pounds of shelled shrimp will be enough or. . . ."

We sat at the table for half an hour, drinking coffee and making the final decisions on the luncheon — shrimp cocktails, yes, an orange gelatin salad, breast of chicken, asparagus, almond sherbet. Cold duck before the luncheon, coffee with it.

I was still ticking things off in my mind as I walked into the foyer with its wide expanse of shining oak floor and two small oriental throw rugs. The carpet in the living room must be vacuumed. I would use the hand sweeper on the rug in the dining room. Flowers. I would need cut flowers. From the garden or the florist? Nicer, of course, if they came from the garden, but last week's rain had rather flattened the chrysanthemums. Perhaps I should call the florist this morning.

I was standing, undecided, one hand on the newel post,

14

when I heard the distinctive click of the front gate. I turned back toward the front door, thinking that I must remember to oil the gate hinges before Wednesday. I opened the front door and watched our postman walk up the flagstones.

"Hello, Mr. Karnes. A beautiful morning, isn't it?"

"Sure is, Mrs. Hamilton." He stepped up onto the porch. "Got a bunch for you today."

And he did. I took the letters, perhaps eight or ten, and glanced through them, noting the several addressed to me. I didn't look too closely because I knew they would be invitations, advertisements, or bills. Not personal letters. I never received personal letters. I tucked the magazines under my arm and turned back into the house.

I paused to look at the grandfather clock. Five minutes after ten now. Margaret would not be out of preschool until eleven-thirty. The morning still stretched agreeably before me, time enough to read the mail, time enough, perhaps, to go by the library on my way for Margaret.

I heard the low hum of the floor polisher as I passed the dining room. Willamae had already finished in the kitchen. I filled a pottery pot with coffee, put it and a cup on a lacquered tray, and placed the mail along one side. Turning back toward the main hall, I walked to the stairs. I ran my hand along the banister as I went up, thinking that a little polish might be a good thing. Upstairs, I turned to my left, my objective the sun porch that sat above the screened-in porch. Of all the lovely places in a house I adored, the sun porch was perhaps my favorite, and it certainly was from mid April to early November. Opening the French doors, I stepped out onto the porch. I scooted a wicker chair a little sideways to the sun, sat down, and reached forward to put the tray on the patio table.

I was alone in a tree-high retreat. The old elm where the

blue jay had scolded Gray Lady shielded the porch from the street, and white-barked sycamores screened it from our nearest neighbor. My only companions were some starlings, chattering and milling about in the elm. The leaves were turning and the maples in the back yard blazed in the sunlight.

A perfect fall morning.

The fall. Unbidden, a picture flashed in my mind of a dusty road and dark cypress trees and a handsome face and strong arms reaching out to hold me. For a moment, a moment stolen in time and space, I remembered Morgan and wondered, with an ache in my heart, where I might be now if we had been fated to stay together. Then, almost angrily, I swept the memory away. The past was done and finished. This was the present and it belonged to Paul and to Margaret.

I reached out with a steady hand and poured a cup of coffee. I drank it quickly, delighting in its sharp heat. It was hot and real and here. I began to pick up the mail, piece by piece. This was now. This was my life. A bill from Grainger's department store. Another from Foss' hardware. Ditto Bank Americard and Texaco. Then I studied a small squarish envelope with my name typed on its face. It intrigued me. It was the proper size, say, for an invitation to a coffee or a tea. But hostesses do not type their guests' names. So, not an invitation. I balanced it on my fingers, then put it aside for last. A letter to Paul from his mother. Two advertising brochures, one touting pink-striped toothpaste, the other an inch-tall radio, the electronic marvel of the century.

I picked up the invitation-shaped envelope again. It had no return address. I turned it over but, no, there was nothing on the back to name its sender. I pulled on the flap, opened the envelope, and lifted out a single square-cut sheet of child's notebook paper. I knew even as I saw that carefully cut sheet of paper that something was more than odd. I held the little square of paper in hands that suddenly trembled, and stared at the words so thickly drawn in black crayon. My breath caught in my throat and my chest ached. I closed my eyes and crumpled the paper in a wad.

But the thick black letters still quivered in my mind, sharp and ugly as a flesh-hung barb.

ANN SEVERIN, YOU KILLED 54 PEOPLE
NOVEMBER 6, 1966

# II

I don't know how long I huddled in the chair and could not stop shaking. All the while I knew that I must think, that I must not cower behind physical fear.

I opened my right hand and stared at the crumpled ball of paper. Slowly, my face drawn and tight, I took the damp wad and carefully opened it up — and still the crayoned letters proclaimed their message.

ANN SEVERIN, YOU KILLED 54 PEOPLE
NOVEMBER 6, 1966

I had not in a mind-bent moment imagined it. No, the dreadful words were there.

I wanted to jump up and rush down the stairs and escape. But there was no escape. Run though I might, the words would still be on that crumpled sheet of paper. The words that meant I had gambled and lost.

What was I going to do?

Six years ago, I had run away. I couldn't run now. What would be the use? Paul and Margaret were all in the world that mattered to me. They were here. My life was here.

If I could not run then I must stay.

Somehow I walked down the stairs and spoke to Willamae, ordered flowers for Wednesday, called the liquor store for cold duck, picked up Margaret at school.

Margaret knew. Oh, not what had happened, of course.

But with the heightened instinct of the utterly dependent small child, she knew something was off balance. She asked what was wrong before the car even neared home. I managed a tight shrug and an "I have a headache, honey." That satisfied her. A headache was a known and understandable blight in her world. But still she was cross when I wouldn't let her play outside after her nap.

"Why?" she demanded.

I didn't know. I only knew I didn't want her out of my sight, not even in the back yard. She finally settled for clay in the kitchen while I did unimportant things and tried to comprehend the end of my world.

What else could it signal? Although why anyone should choose to end it in such a fashion was impossible to understand.

No matter how inconceivable it seemed, the note signaled the failure of a masquerade begun in fear and desperation that long-ago November and continued with faint hope of success and, finally, carried off to a happy conclusion.

I should have known I was doomed to failure. Why hadn't I realized that exposure must surely come some day? When I met Paul and loved him, I should have run away again. How could I have convinced myself that it would be all right to marry him? And now there was Margaret to suffer for the folly of her mother.

Throughout the interminable, nerve-taut afternoon I forced myself to talk occasionally to Willamae, as I had always done. I painstakingly dusted the books in the study and ran the dust mop along the moldings around the ceiling as if the luncheon would occur on Wednesday. Yet all the while I was answering questions in my mind, explaining, defending, denying — pleading.

"Yes, yes, I did use a false passport to return to the United

States that November. Yes, that is true but. . . ."

"Yes, I was using the name Janey Torbet when I first met Dr. Hamilton."

"Yes, I knew my name was included in the fatality list."

The answers were hard but not nearly as hard as the questions.

"Why, Mrs. Hamilton?"

"Wasn't that a lie, Mrs. Hamilton?"

"How much were you paid, Mrs. Hamilton?"

Worst of all, how could I tell Paul? How could I ever tell him?

The fact of the accusation would not hurt him nearly as much as the fact that I had hidden it all away. Could he ever understand that I didn't want to disinter the horror of it? That I had felt not that I couldn't trust him with it, but that I did not want to burden him with a past which I couldn't alter. By the time I met Paul I well understood what a fool I had been and how I had been so neatly and mercilessly used. I also knew that it was too late, much too late, to try and tell anyone the truth of it.

Too late. Yes, it was much too late now.

The phone rang.

I whirled around and the dust mop cracked against the brass lamp on Paul's desk, knocking it to the floor. The bell shrilled again. I took a deep breath and lifted the receiver.

"Hello."

"Mrs. Hamilton, I'm so sorry to bother you. This is Candy Riddell. My husband is Dan. If you remember, Dr. Hamilton introduced us to you at the play last week. And I'm so sorry to have to call, but we're some of the new people, you know, and my little boy, well, he lost the invitation and I didn't know anyone else to call and ask the time. . . ."

Her voice trailed off.

20

I tried to speak and couldn't.

"Oh, Mrs. Hamilton, did I call at a bad time? Or maybe I shouldn't have called at all. I just didn't know anyone. . . ."

Her high, sad little voice was growing shriller and I finally managed to answer. "It's quite all right, Candy, quite all right. I had tangled the phone in my knitting, please forgive me. And I'm so happy to have a chance to talk to you. Please try and come about eleven-thirty. We will visit for a while before we lunch. And don't worry about losing the invitation. Our little girl is four and sometimes she can do the most extraordinary things."

Forgive me, Margaret, I thought. You are a small person most thoughtful of others and their possessions.

"Oh, you have such a little girl!"

Candy's superb gracelessness almost brought a smile to my face, but it was much too late for smiles.

"Yes. And I will look forward to hearing about your son, Candy, on Wednesday."

Yes, I thought, if the hostess isn't in jail, she will be happy to hear about him.

"Oh, we have three, Mrs. Hamilton. Tommy is two and Cindy is. . . ."

The conversation finally ended. I hung up the phone, then knelt to pick up the lamp. The shade was bent but the body of the lamp was sturdy. I set it back on the desk.

It was foolish to have panicked when the telephone rang. They wouldn't call. They would come.

"Why, Mrs. Hamilton?" they would ask.

It was late afternoon. Willamae had left and the shadows stretched across the front lawn when I stepped out to pick up the evening paper from the porch. I watched the paperboy wheel down the street and I realized that I must have mistaken the import of the scrawled note.

Throughout the long day I had awaited a sharp knock at the front door and the sight, sure to interest my neighbors, of uniformed men on my porch, and a patrol car in my drive.

Now I stood on the porch and held the paper, knowing that it was past five o'clock. If the police were coming, wouldn't they already be here?

Then the quick little spurt of hope faded. If they did not come today, they would come another day. I was, after all, a respected member of a small community. They would not lightly accuse the wife of the head of a university department of murder. Even now inquiries were undoubtedly being made to the Italian police, to the passport authorities, to the state of California.

How long before they would come?

I turned around slowly and walked back into the house. It didn't really matter how long it took. The added days would give me no advantage. I had nothing to run to. All that I valued was here.

"Mommy? Mommy?"

"Yes, Margaret."

"Mommy, you promised we would go to the park. You promised."

I nodded. The shadows were thickening now but we had another half hour of daylight. And suddenly I wanted to be out of this house where I had waited in dread throughout the long day. There was no need to fix dinner. Paul was not home.

Would I ever fix dinner for Paul again?

"We haven't much time before it gets dark, but we can go for a little while, honey. Then, if you like, we'll stop at McDonald's for hamburgers."

She clapped her hands in delight. It takes so little to please a child. A few minutes in the park. A hamburger.

"Run upstairs and get your blue sweater, Margaret, then we'll go."

I never regretted that next hour though it meant that night had fallen and Margaret and I were alone in the house before I sat down to read the evening paper, the paper I had so carelessly tossed into the wing chair by the fireplace.

It was almost seven when we got home. Margaret's eyes sparkled in her thin face. She had muddy feet from a patch of damp ground beneath the slide, and sticky hands from her chocolate shake. I carried her up the stairs and to the bath. She poured in a huge mound of pink bubble bath while I turned on the water full force, and then she splashed and played with two tiny plastic sailboats and let me help her soap. When she was scrubbed dry and encased in a fresh gown, she climbed up on her bed and settled beneath the covers while I read her favorite Pooh story, in which Piglet meets a Heffalump. Then I tucked the covers under her chin, kissed her good-night, and turned off the light.

I was almost to the door when her sleepy voice called, "Mommy, what are we going to do tomorrow?"

I turned back and stood looking down at her. God, what was I going to do tomorrow?

"I don't know, honey. I don't have anything special planned."

And she murmured a drowsy sigh and was asleep.

I couldn't bear to stand there looking at her. I hurried out the door and to the stairs. Tomorrow. Would the police come tomorrow?

I stopped midway down the stairs. Could I possibly bluff? If I insisted I was Janey Hamilton nee Torbet, could they prove otherwise?

Fingerprints?

Slowly I walked on down the stairs. Somewhere a record

of Janey's fingerprints might exist. But they might not. I frowned. Heel prints. Wasn't that how they identified babies in hospitals? But hadn't I read somewhere that such prints are useless in adult identification? I didn't know.

They would have a damned hard time getting either my fingerprints or a heel print. I would not willingly permit them to be made.

So, could I bluff?

I flicked on the light in the living room. It was a graceful airy room with two bow windows, a red-bricked fireplace, and comfortable furniture. I walked slowly to the wingback chair and bent down to pick up the paper and carry it to my easy chair. I sank tiredly down into its soft cushions.

All right, I would bluff. They would drag me down, protesting my innocence with every breath. I would not give up easily.

Automatically I began to unfold the paper, rubbing away a smear of dried mud along its edge.

What if the police brought someone to Lancaster who had known Ann Severin in Italy?

Again, I would deny it. So I resembled a blond girl someone had known fleetingly years before in another country? So?

I sat in my easy chair, my hands loose in my lap, the paper open. I was Janey Hamilton, Dr. Hamilton's wife. It had been six years since anyone had seen Ann Severin. Let them prove it.

I sat in the chair, grim faced, staring with unseeing eyes across the lovely room. Let them prove it. I would not help. I would fight every inch of the way.

With that decision, I felt better than I had all day. I wasn't defeated yet.

If they searched long enough, hard enough, likely they

could prove I was not Janey Torbet. Let them try.

Wearily, I glanced down at the opened front page. Trouble in the Middle East. A sharp Russian note to the United States. Inflation up another point. Conference for police officials upcoming on the campus. Announcement that the Israeli Defense Minister will arrive tomorrow to give the annual Morton Leiberling address. Drug raid nets twenty-three students. VD campaign underway.

None of it mattered to me. How unimportant is the world when our own center is threatened. I turned the pages slowly, glancing at photographs, reading an occasional paragraph. I could not have said what it was that I read. Had I been asked, I would have said that I scarcely ever gave the classified pages a glance — yet I saw the announcement immediately. My eyes went directly to it. It was in the Personals column, of course. I had never read the column before, yet I saw it at once.

It was not the same message this time. As I read it, as its weight pressed against my mind, I knew I had made a mistake. A serious miscalculation.

The message was simple, direct.

ANN SEVERIN: VENGEANCE IS MINE

I read and an icy coldness touched me. I had misunderstood entirely the nature of the threat. It was not the police I should fear.

# III

The paper slid to the floor as I pushed up and out of the chair and ran to the stairs. I raced up the steps two at a time and flung myself at Margaret's half-open door. Pushing it back, I ran to her bed. My heart thudding, I clung to the bedpost and thankfully saw the small mound beneath the covers. She stirred and murmured, then was still again.

I must protect Margaret. That was first of all things. I closed the windows, locked them, then paused uneasily again beside her bed. Margaret slept on her back. One hand lay open, palm upward, on the pillow. Such a small hand. I wanted to gather her up, hold her tight, but I knew that for the moment, the windows locked, she was safe enough. Still, it was hard to leave her alone in her room.

I shut her door and stood in the hall, waiting for my heart to stop its frightened thudding. I couldn't hear over the pounding in my chest and I knew I must listen to every sound. I felt that danger was very near.

I looked up and down the hall. Did something move there at the end of the hall in the darkness near the door to the sun porch? God, it would be so easy for someone to climb the old-fashioned square brick pillars, pull themselves over the low wooden railing, step quietly across the porch, skirting the wicker chairs, reach out and open the French door, and walk down the hall. . . .

My eyes ached from the intensity with which I stared into that shadowed end of the hall.

Slowly, unwillingly, I moved down the hall, moved toward darkness. At the head of the stairs was the switch which would turn on the hall lights. I reached the switch and my hand darted up to pull it down.

The lights at either end of the hall glowed to life, spreading pale beams through rose-patterned fixtures, and the shadows melted away like hag-ridden dreams in the morning sun. The lovingly polished oak floor gleamed goldenly. The French door to the porch was closed.

I ran to it and turned its lock, then rested my back against it and faced the long length of the hall again. Each door was neatly closed. There was nothing to strike fear in the shape or form of those doors, ordinary white wooden doors with old-fashioned clear-glass knobs. I knew those doors and knew what lay behind each one, knew them as well as I knew Paul's face, every line and crease from his stubborn chin to the crinkles that fanned out from his eyes when he smiled.

The end door was the most familiar door, our door, our room. The room where we'd created Margaret, the room of our nights. How many nights had I turned that knob so eagerly? Now the blank white panels of the door mocked my knowledge. Did I know what lay behind that door now?

Across the hall was a guest bedroom, a hall closet, another guest bedroom. Empty now, of course. Weren't they?

I stood against the French door and I knew I must walk down that hall and open those doors, one by one.

If danger waited, what would I do?

I hesitated, then walked quickly down the hall to the room just past Margaret's. I didn't hesitate because I knew that wouldn't help. Instead, I turned the knob and shoved the door in hard and turned on the light. It was a cheerful room, my sewing room. The cover of the machine was open and I could see the bright array of spools in their little cabinet. It was just as I had left it yesterday afternoon. There was the tennis skirt I had almost finished. It needed only the stitching around the zipper. I had thought I would wear it the next time I played with Phoebe. Would I ever play tennis again?

The scissors were where I'd left them. I had dropped them carelessly into the easy chair when I'd heard the front door open and known Paul was home from his golf game. I snatched up the scissors, strong shiny scissors of English steel, and turned back to face the hall.

Our room first. I threw back the door and flicked on the light, then looked around the room with the eyes of a stranger, not seeing the heavy white colonial spread on the double bed, or Paul's leather reclining chair beneath the lamp, or the dresser with its array of comb and powder and brush and cologne reflected in the mirror.

Paul's closet door was ajar, mine closed. I walked stolidly to the closets. Paul's clothes hung neatly spaced from the metal rod. His closet always charmed me, the shoes spaced so exactly, the clothes arranged so precisely. I had teased him, wondering how he could make room in his life for two such casual, frippery women as Margaret and I.

I shut his closet with a snap and moved to open my own. There were too many clothes, too many shoes for neatness. What a wealth that closet represented to me. There had been so many years with a hook for my single coat and a drawer for my jumper and panties and socks. Then later, at the university and in Italy, there had been closets but so little to hang in them. My crowded closet meant more to me than Paul had ever known. I shut it with a snap, then moved swiftly to the windows, pulling them down and latching them tight.

Back in the hall, I checked Margaret's room once again.

She slept more deeply now, half on her side, the pillow humped under her chin.

Reassured that Margaret was still safe, I hurried to the guest bedrooms. One was in beige tones, one in the palest of yellows. I had redone the rooms myself. I chose a print of Cezanne's *Still Life with Apples* for the yellow room and Daumier's *The Washerwoman* for the beige room. I had thought them cheerful, welcoming rooms. They held no warmth tonight. They seemed so alien that they could have been rooms at a roadside motel. Each was empty — empty of threat, empty of charm. They were merely rooms to be checked, windows to be locked, one more stop on the road to safety.

That left only the two linen closets, Paul's mother's room, and Margaret's playroom. The closets held no threat. Paul's mother was as fair as he was dark, as exuberant as he was precise. I had planned the room especially for her, a wine-red rug, Polynesian print wallpaper, wicker furniture. She had been pleased with it, I knew. Tonight the light flickered on and the room looked strained and artificial. I wondered if my house would ever seem my own again.

The playroom had smiling-face wallpaper and a bright yellow child's table with matching chairs. I peered beneath the blanket draped over two sawhorses. It could serve as a tent deep in a fir forest or a mountain cave or a dragon's den, depending upon Margaret's fancies. Tonight the blanket sagged lifelessly toward the floor. I locked the three windows and knew the second floor was now secured.

I hurried down the hall once again to the head of the stairs. I stared down the smooth, shining steps and listened. It was terrifying to stand in my own house and feel the silence to be inimical. I took a deep breath and started quietly down the steps. If only I had read the newspaper when it first came!

Then I would have known and I could have moved to protect Margaret. Instead, it was night and we were here alone. Vulnerable.

I reached the landing and could see the entrance hall with its interlocking parquet flooring and the marble-topped table on one side and on it a bowl of bronze chrysanthemums. The modern grandfather clock sat across the entry way and its steady tick tock was inordinately loud to my listening ears.

Step by step I moved down the stairs. At the base, I waited, listening. Something scratched against a window pane in the dining room. I whirled around and stared across that darkened room. For a long moment. I didn't breathe. It sounded again. A tree branch, that was all.

It took longer to check and lock up the ground floor because it was an old house with many windows and doors. I went first to the kitchen and, as soon us the back door was latched, opened the cutlery drawer and exchanged my scissors for a very sharp carving knife.

Finally every window and door was locked, except the front door, and I wouldn't chain it until I was sure the cellar harbored no one. I hesitated at the cellar door. I didn't want to go down into its darkness! I touched the knob, then drew back my hand. Instead, I reached up and shoved shut the bolt which we had added to protect Margaret from the steep cellar steps when she was smaller. If anyone was in the cellar, he'd stay there now.

I locked and chained the front door then sank tiredly into the chair by the hall telephone. For the first moment since I had dropped the evening paper to run frantically up the stairs to Margaret, my house felt safe. Death and hatred might be near, but they were not beside me. For this moment, Margaret and I were safe.

For this moment.

30

What was I going to do? How could I protect us?

I reached out to touch the telephone. Paul, I would call Paul. Perhaps there would be a flight back to Lancaster tonight. He would come and. . . .

Yes, if I called him he would come. What was I going to tell Paul? Honey, someone wants to kill me. Why, he would reasonably ask, why would anyone want to kill you? Paul, I'm sorry, but you see, I'm not who you think I am. Of course you are, he would say, you are my wife, Janey Hamilton. But no one wanted to kill Janey Hamilton. It was Ann Severin they wanted to kill. And I could not tell Paul about Ann Severin. Never, never, never.

Oh yes, argued one part of my mind coolly, you can tell him, Janey. If it is the only way to safeguard Margaret, you can tell him.

What was I going to do?

Quickly, Janey, think quickly, the minutes are running out. Something will happen tonight, else why the notice in the Personals column. Yes, something will happen tonight.

I looked around the hall, the beautiful hall with its well-kept floor and massive front door and archways opening into the living room on one side and the dining room on the other. Beautiful rooms, lived-in rooms with old and comfortable furniture, rooms that tonight wore secret faces, that slipped from easy familiarity to a mocking strangeness, that reminded of lives lived here before of which I knew nothing and deeds to come that I could not control.

The grandfather clock struck the half hour and the low mournful tone echoed in my mind. The minutes were running out.

If I couldn't call Paul, what could I do?

# IV

You call the police when you are in trouble. But a fugitive can't call the police, can't ask for the good offices of the law. I was as debarred from seeking the law as the one who threatened me.

Unless. . . . I frowned in concentration. I turned the idea this way and that and felt the beginnings of a great relief. No matter how I turned it about, I saw no danger to me in my plan. And it should give me a night of safety for Margaret.

Quickly I grabbed up the phone book, found the number, and dialed. It was answered on the second ring. They were obviously efficient public protectors in Lancaster.

I tried to sound nervous and distraught. It wasn't difficult.

"Please. This is Mrs. Paul Hamilton, 982 Franklin Drive. There is a prowler in my yard. I saw him out my kitchen window. My husband is out of town and my little girl and I are here alone and I. . . ."

"We will send a patrol car immediately, Mrs. Hamilton. Is your house locked up?"

"Yes, yes. I just checked all the windows and doors but it's an old house and someone could easily break in."

"Will you hold on for a moment, please."

I waited and heard the cracklings and buzzes in the background, and the faint sound of a conversation with a squad car, and then the bright young voice of the dispatcher came back on the line.

"Patrol Car 8 is on its way, Mrs. Hamilton, and will be there within a few minutes." Then he dropped his impersonal tone. "I wouldn't worry, ma'am. It's probably just a window peeker from one of the dormitories. One's been sighted a couple of times in the last few weeks. He hasn't broken in anywhere, of course. But the patrolmen will look around real good for you."

I thanked him. I had no more than switched on the front-porch light when I heard the ah-waah of a siren and then a car squealed onto Franklin and hurtled the length of the street to careen into our drive.

Had there been a prowler, I think the noise would most effectively have persuaded him to depart — if not to drop dead from fright. But that was all right too. The more noise, the more coming and going, the more unlikely it was that anyone would lurk near the house. Tomorrow the protection would be gone. Unlike Scarlett, I was planning for tomorrow as well as I could.

I waited until I heard the heavy, solid thump of leather heels on the wooden porch before I unlatched and opened the door.

"Mrs. Hamilton? You reported a prowler?"

"Yes, officer. I saw someone from my kitchen window. That way." I pointed toward the drive and the side of the house.

He turned and looked, and shook his head when he saw the thick grove of trees that bounded our lot. "If he went that way, ma'am, I don't expect we'll be able to find him. How far do those trees run?"

"About half a mile. There's a gully. Red Fork creek runs down it. It's wild land all the way to the Tenth Street expressway."

"Well, ma'am, we'll take a look, then check back with you. Don't worry now." He looked absurdly young as he reassured me. The heavy, webbed belt dwarfed his young-man's waist and the gun holstered at his side looked too big to be real. He turned to his partner, an equally young man, and said, "You go around to the west, Charley. Keep your flashlight on so I'll know it's you."

As they moved away, walking heavily through dry, crackling leaves, I was glad for their sake that they faced no danger here. I shut the door and hurried back to the phone. Now I would call Phoebe and ask if Margaret could come and visit for a few days. With five children ranging from two to eleven, what would be one more? My hand was on the receiver when I paused.

Phoebe was open, loving, delightful, gregarious, charming. And her mouth never shut. What could I tell her? Of course I wouldn't really have to tell her anything. She would welcome Margaret without asking a question. But she was utterly incapable of reticence. Anyone with whom she dealt would likely learn of the little friend visiting for a few days.

I wanted no one to know where Margaret was.

My friends. Well, there was Harriet Rjekec down the street. Harriet was waspish and highstrung but basically gentle and kindly. She would welcome Margaret. But no, that was too close to home. Margaret must not be near here. For so many reasons.

Stella Hoover? We were friendly, yes, but Stella was a rather formal woman whom you never felt you really knew well. She would be astounded if I should ask whether Margaret could come and stay.

I held my hand hard against the receiver and faces flashed in my mind. Sally Stein, Pat Ford, Sue Ann Wilson, Hilda Wentz. I realized as I called the roster that for one reason or another I could call on none of them.

A muscle trembled in my lip. What was I going to do? I needed someone to whom Margaret mattered as a person.

Someone. . . . Quickly, quickly, I lifted the receiver and dialed. I had just finished the call when a knock sounded at the front door. I hurried to open it.

The young policeman stood there, frowning. "Ma'am, did you say your name is Hamilton?"

I nodded.

"Yeah, that's what I thought you said. So it's kind of strange. Would you come? I want to show you something funny."

I followed him to the steps, then stopped.

"My little girl is asleep upstairs. I don't want to leave her alone with the door open."

"Oh, yeah," he replied. He turned and looked toward the far side of the house. "Hey, Charley!"

"Yeah, Hank."

"Stay on the porch and guard the door while I show the lady."

"Okay."

I waited until Charley stood by the open front door, then I hurried down the steps and followed the slender young policeman toward the driveway.

I drew my sweater close around my shoulders. It was cold with the chill of a fall night. The big ball of light from the policeman's flashlight speared through the thick shadows beneath the sycamore trees and traced the graveled surface of the drive that led to the separate frame garage at the back of the lot. When we were perhaps ten feet from the garage, he lifted the beam of light until it illuminated the bright white double doors.

I stumbled, then forced myself to walk steadily on.

He was a few feet in front of me so he reached the garage first and held the light only inches from the door.

"Looks like it was done with a spray-paint can. A funny

thing to write, isn't it? Did you buy the house from somebody named Severin?"

I shook my head and answered in a dry, thin voice. "No, officer, we didn't."

"You know anybody named Severin?"

"No. I know no one of that name."

The letters were a couple of inches high, blotched and uneven.

The young policeman shrugged. "Looks like maybe a kid did it. But usually they go in for dirty words." He paused and frowned. "I think maybe we'll check the directory and see if there's anybody around here named Severin. 'Cause it's kind of offbeat."

I stared at the uneven, blotchy, black letters and my heart thudded so hard I was surprised that the young man didn't hear it. Yes, a child could have sprayed that message, but it had been done by no child.

And now I was sure of the message.

The spray paint had shaped a tombstone and within it, glistening in the light of the flash, was the legend:

ANN SEVERIN
MURDERESS

"You're real sure you don't know anybody named Severin?"

I heard his young voice and I wanted badly to cry yes, please, help me. But I could not. Even if the authorities would overlook my less serious breaches of the law (and would they be willing to consider a false passport nonserious?), why should they accept my version of what had happened in Italy? Why wouldn't they indeed consider me a murderess? And even if all these things could be managed and explained and excused, it would all be meaningless because it would mean telling Paul that the woman he married had lied to him about her name, her past. Would it be surprising if he wondered if she'd lied when she'd said she loved him? (Paul, Paul, I love you so much.)

"You thought of somebody?" the young officer asked me eagerly.

I came back from a long way. "No. No, I haven't thought of anyone." I paused. "It is odd, isn't it?"

"Yeah. Well, I guess I better go call in."

"I wonder if you would do me one further favor?"

"Sure, ma'am, if we can."

"Would you be kind enough to check my cellar for me?"

"Why, sure, Mrs. Hamilton."

I knew from his tone that he thought he was dealing with a real nitwit. But it didn't matter what he thought.

While he and Charley unlocked the cellar and clumped down the stairs to shine their flashlights around and about the cavernous room, I hurried upstairs and swiftly packed a small suitcase for Margaret, then gently shook her awake and told her we were going to take a drive.

Sleepy and puzzled, she let me dress her in slacks and a pullover sweater and sneakers. I had her in my arms, her face nestled against my neck, when the young men came up the cellar stairs.

They looked surprised.

"I have decided to spend the night with friends."

"Here, ma'am, let me carry that," and the young officer in charge took the suitcase. His partner muttered something about the radio and lumbered off toward the patrol car, but the young man named Hank waited on the porch while I pulled the big front door shut and locked it. Then, holding Margaret's small case in one hand and his flashlight in the other, Hank led the way toward the drive.

So it was he who was in the lead when we reached the garage. He shifted the little suitcase under his left arm and reached out with his right hand to pull up the overhead doors.

"They are locked," I said apologetically. "We'll have to go in the side door." I handed him my car keys with the Yale key dangling free. I was so accustomed to having a man open and unlock doors that I didn't even think about it.

He smiled and took the key and we moved toward the side of the garage. He put the key in the lock and turned it. Later I wondered whether it had been locked at all, but, of course, who could know?

He twisted the knob and pushed the door in and then everything happened so quickly that it seemed to happen all together, though I know it did have a sequence. First there was the momentary resistance of the door, then the eerie sound of dry seed pods rattling furiously, then the beam of the flashlight stabbed into the ink-black darkness of the garage, and the young officer's arm moved like the flick of a whip, and then there was the deafening violence of a bullet exploding, and the acrid smell of gunpowder.

Margaret's body stiffened in terror and she began to cry, the high, thin cry of a nightmare.

I tried to speak and could only swallow and stare in horror at the shattered head and long twitching body of the snake.

"Man," the young officer said, "that is some snake! Man, that's the biggest diamondback I seen since I almost stepped on one on my grandpaw's farm when I was fourteen. Man, I got him good."

Heavy running steps neared. "Hank, hey, Hank! You okay?" and Charley was with us. Then he too stood and stared at the bloodied concrete floor and the splotched brown scaly body.

Lights were flashing on in the Millers' house behind ours and across the street the front door was opening.

It didn't take five minutes for the neighborhood to gather and for exclamations of horror and excitement and interest to sound.

"Where do you suppose it came from?"

"I'll have to say that living near a creek certainly seems to have its hazards!"

"Now, Mr. Perry, I've lived on this block for twenty-six years and I've never even seen a snake!"

"Officer, it's a miracle you managed to shoot him before he struck you!"

"Oh, Hank's a sharpshooter, all right."

"Just think, Mrs. Hamilton, what might have happened if you had opened that door!"

Mrs. Hamilton had already figured out the answer to that one. And it was ugly. My nemesis was busy. There had been no sign on the garage door when Margaret and I returned from the park. There had been no eight-foot diamondback rattler in the garage, either. I had not been far off when I'd sensed danger that evening. Danger had been very near. Had someone looked in the window and watched as I read the newspaper, waiting with a twisted smile for me to reach the Personals column? Or had it been colder, uglier, more automatic? Had he sprayed the suggestive tombstone, then somehow nestled his death-dealing agent in the garage and slipped off through the night?

If he had waited, the scream of the siren had surely driven him off. For this short space of time I should be able to move unobserved. I should be able to spirit Margaret to safety.

"How fortunate the police were here!" Mrs. Miller exclaimed.

"Mrs. Hamilton reported a prowler . . ." the young policeman began.

"A prowler!"

The exclamations started anew. A prowler. Where and when and what had I seen and where was I going now and had the police found anything? . . .

Of course the odd sign was then displayed.

"Ann Severin," old Mr. Walters ruminated. "No, no one of that name has ever lived here. I grew up in the house just catty-corner there and I'm sure that. . . ."

Finally the excitement dimmed. Margaret had long since stopped crying and now hung limply in my arms, watching, puzzled, still a little frightened. The nice young policeman cleaned up the snake (he was taking it back to the station to show) and I was in my car and backing down the drive. In only a few blocks, Margaret was asleep on the front seat beside me and I was driving steadily and carefully out of town. I was going to be late but I wanted to be sure, very sure, that I wasn't followed.

# V

The early evening traffic was heavy so I couldn't know, really, whether any car followed me. There were always cars behind me. I did my best. I drove unhurriedly to the crosstown expressway but I waited until the last possible moment before swinging hard to my right, wheeling up the ramp and hurtling onto the freeway in front of a diesel truck with just time to spare. Then I used the power of the Mercedes and hummed down the expressway, nipping in and out of the traffic. Just short of the outskirts of town, I swung, again at the last moment, into an exit ramp, squealed down to Twenty-eighth Street, and pulled into a gas station.

While the attendant filled the tank I watched the cars coming off the expressway. None of them slowed, none pulled into the station. The tension in my shoulders eased a little. I pulled out of the station and drove far enough to make a left turn into the expressway ramp, then headed back the way I had come.

I had done my best, and I stopped worrying about whether someone was following. Instead, I drove us quickly and efficiently as I could to the airport. It occurred to me that my telephone might be tapped and my destination already known.

The expressway narrowed to two lanes by the time we reached the edge of town. The traffic was steady but not difficult. At the airport, I bypassed the subterranean lot that served most travelers and boldly drove into an area reserved for airport personnel. It was closer to the main doors. I parked the Mercedes, scooped up Margaret and her suitcase, locked the car doors, and hurried toward the terminal. Once inside, in the shiny, plastic, brilliantly lighted world of counters, maps, and car displays, I felt safe.

At least for a moment. Then the sound of my echoing footsteps and the emptiness of the faces that I'd passed made me hurry my pace and tighten the muscles in my shoulders again. When I reached the American Airlines counter I looked past the familiar face that waited there, and moved near with no gesture of recognition on my part. Then I bent my face to Margaret and said clearly, but not too loudly, "Are you sure you need to go to the bathroom?" Before Margaret could shake her head, I said quickly, "Oh, all right, we'll do that now."

I walked past Willamae and a moment later heard her footsteps following.

Once inside the ladies' room, I set Margaret on the couch and leaned wearily against the plaster-stippled wall.

When Willamae came in I held out my hand. She took it.

I had told Willamae on the phone that I feared a kidnap attempt against Margaret and that I hoped she could keep her safe for a few days. A lie. Perhaps a dangerous one. Willamae would, understandably, be a little puzzled if I hadn't informed the police. But I wouldn't give her time to ask the questions she could reasonably ask.

"The police came tonight," I began.

"Where was a big snake in the garage," Margaret interrupted. "The policeman shot it!"

Willamae looked at me, startled.

I nodded. "Yes. When we came out to the garage, there was a rattlesnake there."

Her surprise gave way to a frown. "You don't find rattle-snakes in town," she said flatly.

"The creek . . ." I said.

She shook her head impatiently. "No, no, not a rattle-snake. A cottonmouth, perhaps, but not a rattlesnake." Willamae, unlike my neighbors, had a mind and used it. But I didn't want her pursuing this.

"I'd better hurry. I don't want anyone to know Margaret is with you."

"Mommy, where are you going?" Margaret's voice was sharp and frightened.

I looked down at her. I had never lied to Margaret. I knelt by her and took her narrow little face between my hands. "Listen, honey, I want you to go and stay with Willamae for a few days. I. . . ." I closed my eyes for an instant, then opened them and said, my voice calm, "I'm going to have to talk to a lot of people and do a lot of things in the next few days and it will be better for you to be with Willamae."

Margaret stared gravely at me. She had never before been told that she was an encumbrance. She didn't know what to say or how to respond.

And I could think of no way to make this sound like a part of the world she knew because it was so different, so unexpected, so disruptive.

Willamae knelt by us and slipped her arm around Margaret's shoulders. "Why, Margaret, you know how many times you've asked to go home with me. Now you will be able to. And it will be very special because we will go and visit my mother who lives on a farm. Have you ever been on a farm, Margaret?"

Margaret shook her head and her eyes brightened. "A real farm? A farm with cows and horses and chickens?"

Willamae smiled and nodded. "One horse, two cows, and

43

lots of chickens. It's only a little farm but you will like it. And guess how many cats live there?"

Margaret thought for a moment. "Two?"

"Seventeen."

"Seventeen!"

"Yes, and they are all kinds, black and white and yellow and gray. Big and little. All kinds."

Margaret was smiling. I stood up, patted her cheek, and forced a smile.

"You have a good time, honey."

Margaret's hand darted out to catch mine. "When will you come for me, mommy?"

"As soon as I can. As soon as I possibly can."

Willamae pulled a crumpled envelope out of her purse, smoothed it, and wrote a detailed description of how to reach her mother's farm. "Six miles east on Highway 87, turn right onto State Highway 14 and go five miles, then turn right onto a graveled road by a country store. Follow this road for about two miles, then turn left onto a narrow track, and it's about half a mile to the house."

Willamae frowned. "It's almost a shack," she began apologetically.

"Do you think that matters to me?" I asked sharply. Then I reached into my purse and pulled out my billfold.

Willamae stood up stiff and straight. "I didn't come to make. . . ."

I interrupted before her misunderstanding could harden into words. "I know that. I know that very well. But you will have to cancel your work for the rest of the week and I don't intend that you should lose that income. People have to eat. And there is no way in the world I could pay you what this is worth to me. You know that."

She nodded slowly but still did not take the money.

I tucked the bills into her hand. "It isn't payment."

"All right then."

It was time to go. The longer I stayed, the more likely it was to bring danger near Margaret. She was curled up on the cheap plastic cover on the divan, watching me and Willamae. She looked small and tired and puzzled.

I wanted to grab her up in my arms and hold her tight. Instead, I leaned over the divan and ruffled her thin little girl's hair and smiled. "Have fun, honey. Pet the horse for me. Do what Willamae says."

Then quickly, quickly, I turned away. "Stay here for a few minutes before you leave, Willamae." I shrugged off my coat, plumped it up on my shoulder so that it looked as if it might cover a sleeping child, and pushed through the restroom door. The coat wouldn't, of course, fool anyone for long, but I didn't need to fool anyone for long. Just long enough to lead them away from Margaret and Willamae.

I turned to my right toward the huge main waiting room and almost ran. If anyone waited, if anyone saw, they would be concerned by my evident speed. I hoped. My flats slapped along the terrazzo floor, sounding indecently loud to me. In fact, few faces turned toward me. The somnambulism so characteristic of airports held weary travelers tight in self-absorption. It was like running, every nerve end quivering with life, through a display of store-window mannequins.

Once outside in the sharp chill of the October night, I ran full tilt. If anyone looked for me, if anyone waited, it was a giveaway. The word rattled in my mind. Giveaway. Dead giveaway. I'd always liked words, liked knowing how a phrase took on a definite meaning that the literal words didn't reflect. Now I ran, a dead giveaway, to gain time for my daughter. To lead the wolf from the lamb. Dead giveaway.

My throat burned from the harsh pull of air down into my

aching lungs before I was halfway to the car but I kept on running, the coat flopping on my shoulder. I scarcely noticed the bus that was pulling up to the main entrance. It stopped and a cheerful group of middle-aged travelers streamed out the front and rear doors.

I thought of them later. If the bus hadn't come then, I would have been almost the only person in that wide expanse of parked cars.

The good-naturedly loud travelers milled about by their bus, watching the unloading of luggage from the side. By the time most of them had straggled inside the terminal, I had reached the Mercedes and unlocked the door, slipped into the driver's seat and pulled the door shut beside me — and locked it. I plumped the coat onto the seat beside me, then moved with furious haste, jamming the key into the ignition, starting the motor with a roar, throwing the car into gear, and pulling away as if my life depended upon it.

In a sense, I hadn't thought it through. I was trying to deal with an unseen enemy who could not, of course, be omnipresent, but I had to act as if he were. Therefore I ran and hurried, trying to lead this phantom away from Margaret. But I suppose in fact, in the second level of consciousness, I judged the menace to be unlikely. Hadn't I maneuvered back and forth on the expressway? Wasn't I really safe for the moment?

The big car moved as slickly as an oiled hinge. Once the lights of the airport fell behind, I began to drive automatically. Now, for the first moment since I had dropped the evening paper to race upstairs to Margaret's room, my mind moved away from Margaret and her safety, moved back to the brutal impact of the anonymous letter, the announcement in the Personals column, and the frightening implications of the paint-sprayed tombstone on the garage door.

The Mercedes sped along the well-traveled road, the main road from Lancaster to the airport. As I drove I forced my mind to face the threat, forbidding it to shade or ease in any fashion the meaning of Ann Severin's resurrection.

Quite simply, quite clearly, someone intended to kill me.

The physical impact was sudden and sickening. Nausea burned in my throat and my chest ached as though I had been physically struck.

My hands tightened on the wheel. I fought away the whirling shape of panic. Five miles, ten, I drove and battled fear.

Suddenly I came up fast behind a lumbering cattle truck. I braked and slowed. I watched the oncoming headlights impatiently but there was never quite enough time and space to pass. The highway began to curve south and I decided to turn off on a country road that we sometimes took to the airport as it ran, in a circuitous fashion, north of town and was closer to our house than the main road.

There was no real reason to be in a hurry but I wanted to get home and think. Vengeance is mine, the typeset line had read. Vengeance.

My face creased in thought. I turned off onto the narrow blacktop and immediately began to pick up speed. After the interminable time behind the cattle truck, the Mercedes seemed to fly. However, I was still driving automatically and forcing myself to think. How could anyone have known to blame Ann Severin? That was impossible to answer. From the Italian police? Perhaps. Although I had fled as much from an inability to face the truth as from any certainty that I was suspected. But I didn't see any other explanation for a threat of vengeance. Vengeance was retribution. I wondered with a cold horror if someone had implacably sought me all these years. There was a viciousness, a determination to destroy that terrified.

The road swooped and curved. My headlights swung across angular, leafless trees and glanced off dark, cold water in a ditch to the right. Then the narrow road topped the crest of the highest hill and began the long run down the other side, for this one stretch a straight and true road.

I hadn't thought about the headlights behind me. Even when the car pulled out to my left and began to gain, I only assumed that the driver wanted to pass. I even eased a little on the accelerator.

The car drew even, then a little ahead of me, and suddenly it began to crowd, riding closer and closer to me. The natural, almost-immediate reaction would be to slow but somehow I knew, even before I swept a quick glance toward the closing car and saw the hulking, shapeless darkness behind the wheel, that I had not feared long enough.

The right hand of the driver began to swing toward me and I knew, too, what that hand held. Before the glass shattered in the window behind me and the buzzing whine of the bullet sounded, the Mercedes leapt ahead as if she had been launched from a catapult.

The Mercedes hurtled down the slope, sixty-five, seventy, seventy-five, eighty, eighty-five, ninety, ninety-five. It was almost as if the car had been built for this moment, like a great jumping champion with legs gathered for the final, mighty leap. I crouched over the wheel and, oddly, felt at ease for the first time since that morning.

Ninety-five, one hundred. The speedometer needle crept now, but crept steadily higher. At one hundred six I felt a lessening of control but still the Mercedes hurtled down the dark road, straight as a cannonball.

The other car hung grimly alongside but I could sense that it was bucketing and plunging. It wasn't built for this.

I was saving my final spurt. At this speed, I wasn't worried about another shot. I knew the other driver needed both hands to keep his car under control. And I knew, too, that in a moment more, soon, soon, the headlights would bore through the darkness and pick up the luminous sign.

Down, down the slope the cars roared, the wild howl of the engines obliterating any other sound. The world had shrunk to the penetrating whine of the motor and the overwhelming feeling of speed, a furious violence rushing headlong through the empty night.

Then the shiny pebbly luminous letters of the warning sign flashed in the headlight beams:

## NARROW BRIDGE

I pushed the accelerator to the floor and the extra thrust gave me a lead of half a car length. I edged to my left a little, just a little.

The bridge then loomed clear in the glare of the headlights, an old-fashioned one-lane bridge with concrete abutments.

Room for one car only.

The Mercedes roared in the fullness of her strength and I began, implacably, to move toward the center of the narrow road. For a heart-stopping instant my pursuer kept straight on. In an instant more, metal would crash and crumple and, at this speed, both cars would spin out of control.

Brakes squealed. The other car rocked and bucked and slowed enough to fall in behind me. We thundered over the bridge and I was in the lead, winning the most important race I would ever run.

Once in the lead, I kept up the pace until the other car had no hope of catching me. Roaring up the other long slope, I topped the crest a good twenty feet in the lead, then saw, dead ahead, a car that seemed to be almost stationary such was my speed. I knew the road began to curve among the hills from this point on. I would have to pass now and hope the road lay empty beyond. I had to pass for two reasons. I could not slow quickly enough to avoid hitting the car in front of me, and I must not slow because my pursuer might try another shot.

I swept around the car that seemed to be sitting still, and saw white faces stare at me. The road was curving now and only the beauty of the Mercedes' balance kept me to the curve, and then I was around the car and safe because the road wound and wound from here to town and my pursuer would never catch me.

But I made no mistake. I did not relax. The battle had begun and would not end until one of us was dead.

# VI

The scream filled the car, edging sharply higher and higher until it broke off in a strangled gasp as the hands, immense hands, hands magnified into obscenity, began to tighten around the girl's neck.

I stared at the huge movie screen and shuddered. It wasn't an omen. I didn't believe in omens — good or bad. This drive-in movie was an excellent place to hide until I had time to collect my thoughts, make some provision for the future, define some course of action.

It had been a last-moment impulse, to pull into the drive-in. As I neared the outskirts of Lancaster, driving as fast as I dared on the curving road, I realized that I couldn't go home. Not unless I intended to sit back and await slaughter. And that was not my plan. However, I had to go somewhere. I couldn't, without raising curious questions, go to the home of friends. I was almost even with the drive-in when I saw its illuminated sign, and it seemed the answer to prayer.

The ticket seller made no comment on the fact that I was alone. Perhaps nothing would surprise him. I found an empty space almost in the center of the grounds, stopped, opened my door to lift the little loudspeaker into my car. Then I reached up and turned off the sound. I didn't want to hear any more screams. I needed to think, hard and fast and well.

It was clear now. Everything fit together into a hideously explicit mosaic. Someone wanted to kill me and at the same time wanted to reveal the truth of my identity. This puzzled me. Would vengeance be incomplete if the world knew only of the death of Janey Hamilton?

Impatiently I pushed the question away. The reason didn't matter. And how much reason did I expect to find in the mind of a man plotting murder?

The crayon-scrawled accusation, the notice in the Personals column, the tombstone spray-painted on the garage door — they had all been stage setting for the rattlesnake, coiled on the cold garage floor, venom in its fangs.

If it hadn't been for the young policeman, I would have opened the door and stepped inside. The rattling sound would have meant nothing to me. Nothing at all. The quivering head would have lifted and lunged forward and struck. When that failed, my pursuer trailed me and tried again. Only the awesome capabilities of the Mercedes had saved me then. So I could be clear on the future. Someone had tried twice to kill me. I must be sure his third attempt was not successful.

Oh, Paul, I am so frightened. I want you here so much. Paul, if I call you. . . . How many lies can a man accept? Would you ever believe me again, Paul, if I told you the truth now? Ever?

If I called Paul, I would lose him. Without him, life would be meaningless. No, I couldn't run to Paul.

Was there anyone who could help me?

Unbidden, a face flashed into my mind. Andrew's face. A tiny core of shock quivered within me. What manner of woman was I that I thought of Andrew? He was new to the university this fall, a new member of Paul's department. I had first met him at a party at Phoebe and John Blair's. I remembered him very clearly.

He had smiled at me and stayed near throughout the party. He had been very charming and I knew I attracted him. A woman always knows. But I treated him as I would any new acquaintance. Nothing more, nothing at all. I seemed to meet him many times in the days to come, and often on the tennis courts. He moved beautifully on a tennis court. His dark eyes followed me warmly. He was fun to play with. We both knew, without saying, that that was all there was to it.

Andrew would help me if I asked him.

I saw his dark handsome face, his sensuous mouth and knowing eyes, and knew I couldn't do that to Paul, either. To turn when in danger to another man, that would be worse than any lie. That would be short only of the ultimate betrayal.

So I would not turn to Andrew.

That left me just as when I'd started — alone. It was up to me. Everything depended upon me. So far, I had moved blindly, driven by fear, first moving to protect Margaret, then ducking into this hiding hole to try and sort out my thoughts.

All right, I was alone. I couldn't go to Paul or to friends or to the police for help. And sooner or later the hunter would find his quarry. He had the advantage. He knew the habitat and coloration of his quarry. He had a weapon.

If he would find me ultimately, if that was the certain outcome, why should I run it out? Why not drive home, walk stolidly up the flagstoned pathway, await the brutal shock of a bullet, hear with fading consciousness the crack of the gun?

I wanted to live.

Insidiously, devastatingly, I remembered others who had wanted to live, who on November 6, 1966, had every reason to look ahead to the next day, the next week, the coming years. I remembered and the old familiar sorrow and despair washed over me. I rested my head against the hard rim of the steering wheel. Did it matter that I wanted to live? What right had I?

I closed my eyes but with my heart I could see Margaret

sitting on the cheap couch in the airport restroom, her small thin face puzzled and uneasy. Then the picture shifted and there was Margaret, vivacious and excited, telling her father about the peacocks at the zoo. He was listening gravely, dark head bent to her.

I lifted my face and stared blindly out at the humped shadows of the cars and the screen with its meaningless splashes of color. Perhaps I had no right. But I had responsibilities.

Now was the moment to choose. I loved Paul and Margaret. For them, I must fight.

All right. I must stalk the stalker. To do that I needed a weapon. I looked at the luminous clock on the dashboard. Twelve minutes before ten.

A weapon. Where in a college town could I find a weapon? No one I knew had. . . . Why yes, of course. John McLeod. He had weapons enough.

All right. I needed a weapon but I also needed some idea of where my danger lay. Before I left the drive-in, before I moved out into the city whose streets were now as dangerous to me as any treacherous path skirting a crevasse, I must try to give some shape and substance to the man who stalked me.

I had been so confident after five years in Lancaster as Mrs. Paul Hamilton. What had happened to link me to Ann Severin?

Something had betrayed me. But what? My days had gone as usual this fall. I always enjoyed the bustle as the semester got underway. Lancaster was once again full of youth and promise, the annual renewal that came as the year began to die. I entertained new members of Paul's department. I helped serve at the tea welcoming new women faculty members and new faculty wives. I was part of the receiving line at the President's Reception, the annual affair for all faculty members. I gardened.

This then was my world. A fascinating, colorful world — but a small one. Perhaps it is true of everyone. How many people, really, does anyone know and see often. Perhaps it is almost certainly true of a woman whose life is bounded by husband, child, home, service.

My days had gone as usual. With perhaps one difference. And I wondered suddenly if it was the Sunday afternoon in the art museum that had betrayed me. That was the only time in my five years in Lancaster that I had gone to the museum, the only time I had ever publicly indicated any interest, any knowledge in art of any kind.

Paul, of course, knew that I saw life in terms of art, that an eerie summer day, hot and still, brought to mind Van Gogh, that a dark and violent storm evoked El Greco, that a somber face reminded me of Rembrandt. But Paul never suspected the truth. He thought it was because of classes I had audited here and reading I had done since our marriage.

My mouth twisted. It would be ironic if that single afternoon had brought down the life I had so carefully built these five years past.

It was a week ago Sunday. Sally Stein had called, breathless with distress. "Janey, please, can you come to the rescue! I know you've already done your part and you did a super job with the advertising. I know you worked like a Trojan on the program, but the whole thing is going to be an absolute bust if I can't get enough people to serve as tour guides, and you won't believe the traumas — a broken leg, children with mumps, a lost father-in-law, a christening, an emergency appendectomy — believe me, Janey, I am out of my mind! Could you please, please work at the museum this afternoon from two to four? It isn't hard, really. There's a printed spiel and anybody could do it, but I have to have somebody there I can trust, I mean to make sure somebody doesn't stuff something into their knitting bag. Those dammed tiles are worth a fortune and it was really a big thing to wangle a showing of the exhibit here in Lancaster. Please, Janey."

I hesitated for just an instant. I had schooled myself for so long never to go near the museum, but, five years safe, I thought it would be all right. And I wanted to see the exhibit. It was on loan from the Metropolitan and it was one of the finest showings of medieval mosaics to tour the United States. Our women's group had arranged for the showing and we were charging a dollar entry fee, the proceeds going to the children's hospital.

I went and I loved it. And I didn't use the spiel. I knew more about the mosaics than whoever wrote the spiel. I led the groups through every twenty minutes and it was fun. I saw so many people I knew. Scads of women, of course, others who had helped on the drive. Members of Paul's department, Tom Brady and Mitchell Hall and old Dr. Abernathy. Andrew. Julian St. Clair, Paul's oldest friend on the campus. The Carmichaels. The Blairs. And, of course, there were many people I didn't know.

Was it at the art museum that a face had smiled at me, a face concealing hatred and anger and a lust for vengeance?

Was it the face of a friend or of a stranger?

My hands trembled ever so slightly before they tightened on the silent wheel. All right. Yes. I was afraid. Dreadfully afraid. But I mustn't let the fear overpower me. I must face the fear and push beyond it, and out of the past few weeks pull the face that mattered, the face that wanted me dead.

The car door opened so suddenly I would have screamed, but the fear that ballooned in my chest left me with no voice to cry out.

# VII

"I thought it was you," he said softly. "The light from the concession stand touches your hair. There is no other hair like yours. It gleams more softly than gold."

"Oh," I sighed in relief. "It's only you, Andrew."

He began to slip into the seat and, after a moment's hesitation, I moved over and he was behind the wheel and closing the door. "Who did you wish to come?" Then, before I could answer, he said, "I know, of course. You wish for your husband, as would any good wife."

I looked at him sharply, hearing the faintly sardonic note, wondering what he really meant, realizing suddenly that anyone seeing us together at a drive-in would think. . . . "Andrew, you must leave. There are students here, of course. It won't do. They might . . . misunderstand."

He laughed at that and I could see the gleam of his teeth in the half-light. "No, Janey, they would not misunderstand at all." He moved closer to me and his arm slipped behind me along the top of the seat.

"Andrew, no!"

His arms were around me and his face was close to mine. "You are a beautiful woman. And your husband is a long way away tonight. Why should you be lonely?"

Until then I was torn between anger and embarrassment, but with that absurd and synthetic appeal, I began to laugh. I felt his body stiffen and then abruptly he pulled me close and tight, his hands were on my neck and his mouth pressed harshly against mine. I was so startled that for an instant I made no response at all. Then, knowing disdain to be very effective, I went absolutely limp.

He tried. He tried hard. And if I hadn't been a woman very much in love with her husband and with problems much more pressing than a problematically lonely night, he might have succeeded.

He was angry. When he pulled back from me, his hand curved about my throat and his fingers pressed hard.

"You could drive a man to dangerous lengths, Janey."

I didn't laugh this time, but my voice mocked him now. "Don't you think you are overdramatizing a bit, Andrew? You know as well as I. . . ."

And then I heard clearly a voice raised in the next car. "I'll bet you it is too Mrs. Hamilton! And that's not Dr. Hamilton with her, either! It's. . . ."

Another voice hissed, "Shh! Can't you shut up!"

I didn't turn to look. It didn't matter who it was. I knew that I could explain this to Paul — if I ever had a chance to talk to him again. In ranking my problems, this one had to be at the bottom of the list. But I wondered suddenly about Andrew. How had he found me here and why had he so gracelessly pawed at me? Could he possibly have noticed some students from the department in the next car and purposely set out to compromise me? I pressed my hands briefly against my eyes. Damn it, nothing made any sense, nothing at all. I only knew I was losing time and once again the sense of pressure and danger swirled around me.

"I think you've caused enough damage for the moment, Andrew. Get out."

He spread out his hands, palms up, and shrugged, but I could hear the laughter in his voice. "As the proverb so wisely suggests, dear Janey, you might as well be hanged for a sheep as a lamb."

I shook my head. "I think, Andrew, you will find that perseverance is more helpful in business than in love affairs."

"Perhaps," he said mildly. He opened the car door and began to slide out. When he stood beside the car, he bent down to look at me. "Are you going home?"

I hesitated and once again wondered about Andrew. His voice was just loud enough, clear enough, to be heard in the nearby cars. And I had no doubt that curious ears strained to hear. No doubt at all. And why should Andrew want to know where I was going?

"Where else would I go?" I asked finally.

"I will be at my apartment," he answered obliquely.

"Good night, Andrew."

I turned on the motor as he closed the door of his own car and began to back out. I hesitated at the drive-in's exit, then pressed down hard on the accelerator and the Mercedes leapt forward. The hunter surely couldn't know that I had hidden at the drive-in. Now I should be safe enough to try to even the odds, to prepare for the inevitable moment when my pursuer and I faced each other again. Next time it would be on my terms, I hoped. In any event, the odds would be bettered when I had a weapon.

The traffic was light as I drove back into Lancaster, heading for the campus. The McLeods lived close to the campus, too, only three blocks or so from our house. I made care to approach from the direction opposite our house.

As I drove, my mind kept flickering back to Andrew. Would he try to follow me to see whether I went home? I didn't think so. But I wouldn't chance it. I took an extra fifteen minutes, making sure I wasn't followed, stopping, starting, circling blocks.

And all the while I wondered about Andrew. Could his be the face of the hunter? Surely not. Why during the crisp electric days of the fall would he so clearly invite me to fall in love with him if he wanted me dead? I had not mistaken his intentions. I was certain of that. Positive. So it couldn't be Andrew.

Besides, if it were he who had tried to shoot me off the road, why then would he follow me to the drive-in and try to make love to me?

Because, a cool, still voice answered, he was already in the car with you, his hands on your throat, before he saw the students who knew him in the next car. If they hadn't been there. . . . It would surprise no one in a drive-in to see a tight embrace and then for the lovers to slip down upon the seat, out of view.

I was driving back across town now, once again nearing the campus.

Was it Andrew? Wasn't it?

I would think more about Andrew later.

# VIII

A single light glowed dimly in the front hall of the McLeods' house. I drove slowly past the two-story frame. No car was in the drive, but it might be in the garage.

Did the single light mean that Professor McLeod and his wife weren't home? Or did it mean they had already gone to bed?

I drove on, realizing that I couldn't just park along the curb. This was a quiet street of family homes. A strange car might easily be noticed. Someone might look down from an upstairs window and say, "Hmm, I wonder whose Mercedes is parked in front of our house?" Then, if lights flashed on and voices called and a running figure slammed into the car, well, a noticing person might get the plate number.

Did an alley run behind the McLeods' house? But even as I wondered I knew it would be a mistake. It would be so easy to be trapped in an alley. I picked up speed and turned the corner. I checked the clock on the dashboard. Ten fifty-two. Not late in a college town. I headed toward the campus proper. Two blocks away the university's belltower thrust up into the night sky, illuminated by spotlights. A solitary walker would not occasion notice on or near the campus.

I parked the Mercedes in the faculty lot behind Felson Hall, which housed the English department, Paul's department. The Mercedes had a faculty sticker, of course. After I dimmed the lights I looked carefully around the lot, waiting for my eyes to adjust to the darkness. There were nine or ten other cars. It was dim in the lot, the occasional lampposts affording only circular splashes of light. The night sky was overcast, thick black clouds hanging low. The wind was erratic, now whipping the almost-bare branches, then subsiding. A boy and girl passed nearby.

When they were out of sight, when I saw no one, heard no one, I slipped out of the Mercedes, locking it. I hesitated for a moment, holding my purse, then hurried to the trunk, opened it, and locked my purse inside. I dropped the keys into my pants' pocket so that I could move unencumbered.

I walked briskly away from the car. It didn't take quite five minutes to reach Linwood Lane, the wide, respectable street where the McLeods lived.

A gusty little wind skittered papers against the curbing. The night smelled of the death of summer and a coming rain. Hurrying, I hunched against the sharpness of the wind. Just short of the McLeods' and mercifully far from the streetlamps, I stepped into the shadows of an immense evergreen.

Abruptly, the high, sharp bark of a terrier broke the quiet. I pressed against the prickly evergreen, damning all dogs and especially the terrier. I could hear him very clearly. His barks rose to a shrill frenzy. He was in the back yard next to the McLeods'.

Pressed hard against the tree, I watched lights flash on in the terrier's house. The side door opened.

"Ginger! Ginger, stop that barking!"

I began to breathe again. Apparently, Ginger had cried wolf too often. Or, more likely, she felt it her duty to warn the world of gophers, squirrels, cats, rats, children, and prowlers, treating each with fine impartiality.

"Ginger! Hush, you fool dog. There's no one out there. Hush."

The terrier yapped harder.

"Oh, come on, get in here."

The screen door squeaked open, claws clicked swiftly across the cement walk and up the steps, the door shut, and the light flashed off.

I didn't hurry now. I watched the McLeods' house. At the end of five minutes, I felt sure that either no one was home or everyone was already abed. The only light shone in the front hall. All other rooms were dark. No sound came from the house or yard. It was utterly quiet, the only sound the creak of tree limbs in the wind.

Moving from shadow to shadow, I slipped across the front yard to the far side of the McLeods' house, as far from Ginger as possible. The McLeods' driveway was the old-fashioned, two-cement-strip kind. I walked soundlessly in my sneakers up one cement band to the back of the house. No fence barred the way so, happily, no dog. At the back steps, I climbed slowly up the wooden treads and tried the back door. It was locked.

Then, for the first time, the enormity of what I was going to do struck me. Could I, Janey Hamilton, actually break into someone's house? My God, what if they were home, asleep, and woke to find me in the darkness of their hall?

I stood on that small back porch and tried to stop trembling. I shivered from head to foot yet my face and hands felt hot and clammy. I gripped the wooden railing by the steps and held on with all my strength, held on and made myself remember Margaret and Paul. I had to do this. For them. Gradually the trembling stopped. I took a deep breath and began to study the back of the house, frowning in concentration, recreating in my mind the interior of the house as I had last seen it, during the previous year's Christmas holidays.

It had been snowing that night and the great flakes had

softly floated down, gently covering the ground, piling up in drifts against the house. We had stepped inside, shaking our coats and laughing, our faces bright with redness from the sharply cold night air. Mistletoe hung from a brass lamp in the hallway. A braided scatter rug caught up the wet clumps of snow from our boots. I let down the hem of my long dress and took Mrs. McLeod's hands in mine, saying how happy we were to come.

The long dresses swirled with color that night. We moved from group to group, talking, hearing phrases from before and behind, caught up in the accelerated pace of a party, speaking quickly, listening intently.

The party began in the living room, spilled over into the dining room, clotted for a while around the buffet, spread back into the living room. It was nearing midnight when I stepped back a pace from the circle which was so vigorously dissecting the relevancy and efficacy of street schools and began to look for Paul. I was ready to go home.

I didn't see him in the living room. Turning, I stepped into the front hall. Lights gleamed in the next room and I saw the ceiling-high bookcases and stepped inside, knowing that it was Dr. McLeod's study. Books filled two walls. I looked to my left and was, for a moment, shocked. The wall above the massive mahogany desk was covered with glass cases and the cases were full of guns, all sorts of guns. Rifles and handguns glistened beneath their glass covers. All were well oiled, obviously handled often. No dust clung to the gleaming black steel of the huge rifle that was obviously in the place of honor. It looked quite capable of felling a rhinoceros.

Perhaps, if you love guns, the cases would affect you differently. I do not love guns. I found it a fascinating but repellent display. There is something inherently awesome in a machine that kills so efficiently, that is designed specifically

64

to pierce the flesh of men and animals.

I stared at the ridged grip of the Luger in the right hand middle case. It was the only weapon I knew by name, but such is the impress of the Third Reich that almost any American over the age of twenty knows immediately and without any doubt the name of that gun.

"Ah, Mrs. Hamilton, so you admire my collection?"

I swung around, startled, and found Dr. McLeod close to me. Closer than I cared for him to be. So close I could see the red flecks in the whites of his shallow brown eyes and the reddened splotches of broken blood vessels on his jowls, and smell the thick mixture of bourbon and cigarette smoke that clung to him. He smiled heavily but there was no humor or warmth, only the automatic obeisance to social mores. I found him as repellent as his armory but, stepping back a pace from his heavy reeking body, I smiled pleasantly and said noncomittally, "I didn't know you were a gun collector, Dr. McLeod."

He moved a step closer. I felt the hard edge of his desk against my back. I slipped a little to my left and stepped back into a square of space between the desk and the wall. The space was only large enough for one.

For an instant his flash of anger was almost palpable, then he again smiled his heavy, meaningless smile and blocked my way, leaning forward to touch with one hand the Luger's case.

"Did you notice this one, Mrs. Hamilton?" his hoarse voice scraped at me.

I stared at the gun, a shiny blue-black, and thought it as evil-looking an object as any I'd ever seen.

"Yes. Yes, I noticed the Luger."

"You won't guess where it came from?" His worn, used voice was pleased.

I shook my head.

"From Hitler's bunker," he trumpeted.

I looked at the pistol and thought its vaunted pedigree as unlikely as the implication that the good Dr. McLeod was in the vanguard of Patton's Army. I knew, as a matter of fact, that Dr. McLeod had been attached to the occupation forces as part of the official historian's staff, but I didn't care enough about the man or his gun to make a direct response.

Then his arm brushed against me and I pressed back hard against the wall. Blandly he said, "Excuse me. I have to get the key so I can show you." He pressed against the decorative wood carving on the side of the Luger's case. The stem of a carved pineapple suddenly separated from the body of the fruit, revealing a shallow depression which held a small silver-colored key.

Dr. McLeod took the key and unlocked the panel of the Luger's case. With great care, he lifted out the gun. He showed me more than I wanted to know about the Luger, how to load and unload it, how to free the safety, how to aim it. And all the while he extolled its qualities, a semiautomatic recoil-operated pistol with an eight-round magazine, powerful and accurate.

I remarked that one wouldn't expect to find a fully loaded gun in the cabinet in someone's den, and asked whether it really worked. He couldn't wait to tell me how well it worked, how beautifully balanced the Luger was, what a superb weapon it was.

At the time, nearing midnight on a snowy December evening, it was a tedious, somewhat irritating end to a party and I was so grateful when Paul ducked through the doorway and lifted his hand, smiling at the relief in my eyes.

But now, as I stood on the top step of Dr. McLeod's back porch, I was grateful for that odd moment in time, grateful too that I had listened politely to his spiel.

The wind was strengthening. It was from the north now, and cold. The tree limbs rustled and bent. The rain would not be far behind. I should delay no longer.

The windows to my left would open, from my memory of the house, into the dining room. The nearest window to my right would give me entrance to the kitchen. Most probably it would open over the kitchen sink. I climbed up onto the wooden railing of the porch, leaned awkwardly over, put one knee on the sill, and gave a push to the window. It moved, then stuck. But it had moved. I pushed and shoved on that window and grudgingly, slowly, it moved up. When it was about halfway up, I stopped and gingerly poked my head inside to listen.

Over the rustle of the trees and the whine of the wind, I could hear a clock ticking, the hum of the refrigerator, and a faint cooing noise that I strained to identify and finally decided must be the wind whistling in the eaves.

It was as dark as a bat's wing at midnight inside that kitchen. I teetered on the window sill and tried vainly to see, but I might as well have worn pirate's patches on my eyes. Hesitantly I swept my hand to my right and felt the end of a kitchen cabinet and, temptingly, a light switch. For a light above the sink? I started to switch it on, then stopped, remembering Dr. McLeod and his brutal, heavy face and sensual delight in guns. He would love to shoot a prowler climbing in his window. Love it. Then I realized that I had long been visible, framed in the window against the somewhat lighter background of the night, had anyone been in the kitchen. So, with a feeling of fatalism, I flicked the light on and, almost immediately, off again. In that one tiny instant my eyes swept thoroughly across the kitchen.

Mrs. McLeod's housekeeping habits were a boon to the housebreaker. No dishes balanced precariously in her sink.

The drainboard was clean and bare. With a great deal of effort, I wiggled feet-first through the window. Once inside, crouched by the sink, I paused again to listen and found it hard to hear over the thudding of my heart because I was well and truly in jeopardy now. There could be no explaining my presence here.

I was at one with the common housebreaker. And then a new fear swept over me. Fingerprints! I had touched the window, the light switch, the cabinet! How inept! Not even the youngest vandal would make such a mistake. I quickly jammed my hand into my coat pocket, hoping, and there, rolled into a ball at the bottom of the coat, was a pair of gloves. Sweat trickled down my face as I yanked on the gloves, then turned back to the sink and fumbled until I found a dish towel. I polished the window, leaning back out to get the outside, and the cabinet and the drainboard, then I shut the window and rehung the towel.

I crossed to the back door, hands before me to find the way. I reached the door, slid open its bolt and turned the knob, pulling the door ajar. Now I had a way out.

Turning, I tiptoed to the swinging door that led from the kitchen. Easing it open, I welcomed the pale glow of the hall lamp. I waited for a moment, listening. The tick-tock of the clock was louder now. The wind rattled a tree branch against the roof. The house was oppressively hot and smelled of lemon oil and camphor.

Finally I felt sure that no one was home. The house had the hollow feel of emptiness. Still, I moved very softly up the hallway.

The door to the study was open. I stepped in and hurried to the gun cases. Once again I stood in that small square between the desk and the wall. I reached up and pushed the stem of the wooden pineapple.

It didn't move.

I pushed harder. Harder. The stem was as immovable as welded steel.

I breathed deeply and tried to remember exactly what Dr. McLeod had done. He had pushed, hadn't he? I tried to recreate in my mind that moment when Dr. McLeod's stubby hand, thickly haired on the back, had reached up to the carved wooden pineapple.

Yes, he had pushed.

I gripped the stem with thumb and forefinger and pushed to the right. Then to the left. There was not even the tiniest give. So, I was not doing it right. I rubbed the back of one gloved hand against my face.

The stem would, of course, move along a predetermined path. It would move easily along the proper course. I gripped the stem again and this time pushed it gently up a notch, and was rewarded by the smallest of clicks. I had found the path. The stem moved up an eighth of an inch, then slid smoothly and easily to the right, revealing the shallow depression and the small shiny key. I grabbed the key and reached up to the padlock on the Luger's case — and heard a car turn into the drive.

I held the key steady, inserted it and turned, and the padlock opened.

Car doors slammed.

I unhooked the padlock from the staple and pulled the hasp to open the case front.

Footsteps sounded on the cement walk leading to the front door.

I pulled open the case, reached in, and grabbed the barrel of the Luger. I pulled. But the gun didn't move.

Shoes scuffed on the front porch.

My fingers scrambled frantically at the band of elastic that encircled the handgrip. I hooked the elastic and pulled it out, and caught the Luger as it slipped free.

Then, without pausing for an instant, I whirled around and dashed across the study to the hall. I could hear the creak of the screen door opening.

I ran.

Pushing through the swinging door into the kitchen, I jumped for the partially open door and flung it open. I heard the front door open and Dr. McLeod's rasping voice as I jumped down the steps and ran toward the drive.

# IX

It is easier to start running than to stop. I wanted to keep on running more than I had ever wanted to do anything. I heard Mrs. McLeod call excitedly, "John! John, come quickly!"

I pushed through the stand of evergreens that separated the McLeods' lot from their neighbor's. Once through, I stopped running even though I could hear Dr. McLeod thudding down his back porch.

I walked softly toward the street, deep in the shadow of the evergreens. As I neared the sidewalk, I yanked off the gloves and stuffed them in my pocket, on top of the Luger. I smoothed my hair, then stepped onto the sidewalk and began to stroll quietly up the street.

Behind me I could hear muffled, indistinct shouts and thrashings in the bushes.

I walked unhurriedly, forcing a thin, high hum through a painfully dry throat. The hum wasn't intended to bolster my courage. Rather, it was a brake on feet that wanted so badly to run. Somehow, you can't run and hum at the same time. So I hummed and tried to saunter, listening all the while to the faint sounds which were so meaningful to me. I walked, a woman out for a late-evening stroll before the storm broke. That was what I would say if someone asked. But with the weight of the Luger hard against my leg, I didn't especially want to be asked.

When I reached the end of the block and turned the corner, I began to walk more quickly. Now I was taking a brisk outing rather than a stroll. The wind was whirling the last of the autumn leaves from the trees and lightning flashed repeatedly in the north. I was glad when I reached the campus because I knew the storm was coming soon.

When I reached the Felson Hall parking lot, I realized that I hadn't thought beyond getting a weapon. When I got into the Mercedes, where was I going to go?

Not home, certainly not home. And I had already decided I couldn't go to a friend's house without raising too many unanswerable questions. Where can you go in a small town in the middle of the night? A hotel, certainly. Yes, I would check into a hotel. Then I was at the edge of the lot. I hesitated and stepped back into the shadows.

The sleek black Mercedes was all alone in the lot now, alone and terribly noticeable. I would be spectacularly noticeable, too, if I walked out into that empty lot.

I didn't dare retrieve the Mercedes or my purse from its trunk until tomorrow, when the campus was full of students and cars.

I couldn't walk downtown to the hotel. Where could I go? An all-night movie? There was one within walking distance. But I shrank from going to that kind of movie house. What kind of trouble might a woman alone find there? It wasn't far short of midnight now. I must find a place to spend the night. I looked out from beneath the evergreen and saw the light spreading in a cheerful pool in front of Felson Hall.

I thrust my hand into my pocket. Yes, there on my key ring were keys to Felson Hall and to Paul's office. I would be safe there, safe as in a vault. Only members of the department and senior clerical staff had keys. Once I made it to his office, no one could get to me.

I worked my way around the building, staying in the shadows, away from the pools of lamplight, until I reached an unobtrusive side door which opened onto unlighted steps that ran down to the basement and up to the first floor. Once inside, I stood on the landing and felt unutterably weary. I slumped against the wall and for a moment the tension and fear slipped away from me.

Overhead ran the pipes carrying heated air, and their warmth made the basement a sharp contrast to the cold, gusting wind outside. The heat, darkness, and musty-stale air combined to make me feel light-headed. Nothing seemed quite real, the warm darkness, the jacket now heavy against me, the discomfort of the Luger's barrel jabbing against my thigh, the odd, high buzz of the furnace.

I don't know for how long I rested there, unthinking, my mind suspended in the warm darkness. Then, abruptly, the freight elevator rumbled in its shaft, not twenty feet away, and it shocked me into movement. At that moment I understood so well the frantic, mindless instinct to flee of the startled small animal.

I hurried up the stairs and reached the door to the first floor before the freight elevator settled in the basement. I hadn't expected anyone else to be in the building this late and once again I was afraid.

It was utterly dark on the first floor but I knew this building. I padded quietly to the main stairs and started up, one flight, two, three. Paul's office was in the front center of the third floor. Felson Hall was an old building, which meant that it lacked a good many amenities, such as central air-conditioning and, in the winter, the heat was fitful. But it had its own pseudo-Gothic charms, including battlements and a central tower that rivaled the Union's. And, helpfully to me, the office windows were hung with red plush drapes.

I felt such a rush of relief to reach Paul's office. I would be safe here. I locked the doors behind me as I passed through the secretary's office and into Paul's inner office. I drew the drapes before I turned on a small lamp.

Thunder rumbled and once lightning crackled very near and I wondered if another corner of the belltower had been struck. It was just past midnight when I settled into the soft, brown leather chair near the windows.

I held the Luger loosely in my hands and stared down at it, then carefully loosened and checked the magazine. It was full. I pushed it in, hefted the gun, and aimed it at a plaster bust of Thoreau. My arms in order, I lay the gun on the table.

Thunder clapped again and again, then rain began to splash against the windows, rattling the panes. How appropriate it was that I should be resurrecting Ann Severin in the rain.

Ann Severin.

I had pushed the very name out of my thoughts these last years. It is incredible how the mind can be trained. I had become Janey Torbet, then Janey Hamilton to my very roots. I did not even hear the name Ann when it was called in a room. The name meant no more to me, heightened my breath, caught my ear, no more than did Katy or Susanna or Eloise. Ann Severin did not exist.

Now, as the rain drove against old bricks, turning the world sodden and cold, stirring deep atavistic fears of darkness and storms, I had to remember.

Rain. Somehow it always seemed to be raining in my memories of the orphanage. Those memories I had kept, furnishing Janey Torbet with Ann's old background. Looking out a window into the rain. Watching thick gray-black sheets of rain sweep across the hard-packed dirt of the playground with its meager stand of swings. Nine swings. Two hundred and seventy children. Watching stolidly in the recreation room as all the blocks and games and little cars were claimed by stronger, scrappier children.

Perhaps that was why Ann Severin read so much. Other memories there. The matron scolding, pulling a book away, insisting it was bad to read too much. But by then the long-legged little girl had learned that a grander, more exciting, incomparably lovelier world was hers within the covers of books. She read day and night, every moment that was not forcibly claimed by others. And, along the way, another miracle happened. A teacher, Miss Neville, opened the world of beauty. Art became not a word but a way of life to Ann Severin.

Oddly enough, the little girl was not an artist, had no particular gift of creation, but she could understand colors and shapes and styles. So the thin, serious shy girl grew up to be a withdrawn but courteous student and her marvelous knowledge of perspective and balance, pigment and texture, theme and focus excited admiration and interest and, finally, a scholarship to the state university.

How many would remember Ann Severin at the university? Few. Very few. Dr. Aaronson. Miss Cooley. Perhaps Dr. Hoke. They would remember, perhaps, her impressive scholarship, her sure instinct. But would even they be able to picture a face after all these years? Perhaps so, since they, of all people, remembered visually, graphically. Ann Severin, a thin-faced girl grown to grave beauty, had moved quietly through her days there, withdrawn, intense, and almost totally inexperienced in human contact. Ann Severin, profoundly grateful for the opportunity to be at the university, spent her hours and days studying, learning, mastering her field. She rarely thought of anything else. She never squeezed into a car, its top heavily laden with skis, to spend a sun-spangled weekend on the slopes. She never sat for hours in the dimness of the Union beer garden, caught up in the delight of arguing cherished viewpoints.

When Florence happened, it was unbelievable — and she had no preparation. That she, Ann Severin, should walk in the city of da Vinci, Michelangelo, Dante, Boccaccio, Donatello, Giotto, was so beyond her experience and her expectations that anything seemed possible and nothing impossible.

The dome of the cathedral, the red-tiled roofs, Donatello's *Judith* and *Holofernes* in the Piazza della Signoria, warm bright days, mandolines, tart red wine, Giotto's *Campanile*, sunning cats on centuries-old steps, Morgan with his gentle hands and flashing smile — the magic never stopped.

Ann's scholarship funds ran to a tiny third-floor room in, to her, an incredibly ancient house not far from the Uffizi Gallery. She met other students, Americans, Germans, French, Danes, Greeks, Italians. She felt at home, part of a group, accepted as she had never been at the university. Part of it was the magic of Florence, the feeling that in this beautiful city, she too must be beautiful. In her thoughts, her view of herself, she was made greater by the glory of Florence. For the first time, she looked out to other people, the English girl, Judith, with her clipped speech and kind manner; Gerhardt, the intense Berliner, and Morgan, the ebullient, charming American.

I had pushed Ann Severin and her destruction so far back in my mind that I now thought of her as "she." But as I huddled in the brown leather chair and let the forbidden pictures flicker in my mind, it was almost as though it were yesterday and I could reach out and touch the sun-warmed fur of Mrs. Giovanetti's cat on the window sill, smell the bread baking at the little panetteria down the street, and hear the rattle of bottles in the metal basket of the milkman's bicycle.

And I remembered Morgan so well. Even when I had ruthlessly repressed Ann and her memories, I had never forgotten Morgan. I loved Paul, yes. But I had loved Morgan first.

I rested back in the chair and was shaken by the sadness and longing that swept over me. Oh, Morgan, I still miss you so! I knew it was folly to think of him, but it was an exquisite pleasure, too, to remember the curve of his cheek, his wiry, thick reddish-brown beard and sideburns, his brilliantly blue eyes. He would walk into a room and the sunlight came with him.

Incredible as it had seemed to me then, Morgan, handsome, desirable Morgan, had sought me out right from the first. As hazy beautiful September days slipped into October, he took me for long walks in the Boboli Gardens, for leisurely dinners in tiny, dimly lit cafes, for moonlight strolls alongside the placid Arno.

How long had it taken me to fall in love with Morgan? A day, two days, a week? To fall with the headlong passionate abandonment of a late first love. I loved to touch his red-gold hair, to trace the line of his jaw, to feel his heart beating next to mine.

And he had loved me in return. I knew it. If only he had been in Florence that final day, I could have run to him.

(*Could you, Ann?* whispered a small doubting voice. *Are you sure?*)

Yes, yes, yes. Morgan was in Amsterdam. He didn't know!

(*He could have known,* that dark, soft voice insisted. *He could have asked you out, made love to you as the first move in an intricate plan to be culminated on November 6, 1966.*)

I did not believe it. I would not believe it. Morgan had loved me. His eyes had been soft, his hands gentle, his mouth warm. He would not have deceived me. He was as much a victim as I.

It was on a Tuesday afternoon, the first week in October,

that I rode behind Morgan on his motorcycle out to the old walls near the Belvedere Fortress. We parked the machine in the sparse shade of an olive tree and clambered awkwardly up to sit atop the old wall. We could see the red-tiled roofs of Florence glinting in the sunlight and the curving golden Arno flowing placidly.

We sat side by side, our legs dangling, and Morgan's thigh was warm against mine. He was in high good humor and our laughter rippled like the leaves of the olive trees in the gentle breeze. He was his most ebullient self. Had I heard about the scandal when Professor Antonini cornered the little blond Danish girl in the supply closet and she escaped by dropping a frame on his foot? Did I want to go to the party that Joe Tom and Billy, America's Gay Libbers in Florence, were throwing for their friend Charles, who had a show opening in Brussels next week? It would be quite a party. Joe Tom liked to dress all in gold leaf and toward the end of the evening climb atop a table and strike a muscled pose.

What a happy afternoon. We laughed and talked and kissed and I wanted to stay there forever, but the sun began to slip down in the sky and the air turned cooler. It was almost time to go when Morgan looked at me searchingly, then asked, hesitantly, "Ann, listen, can you keep a secret?"

Captivating words to any ears.

"A secret, Morgan? Of course."

"Guess where I'm going tomorrow?"

"Rome?"

He shook his head and I kept trying. "Venice? Perugia? Assisi?" I gave up finally. "Where, Morgan?"

"Athens."

"Oh, Morgan, how wonderful! How marvelous! Oh, I wish I could go."

He caught my hands in his. "Why don't you come, Ann?

We could meet there. We can't travel together but. . . ."

He broke off as I shook my head.

"I just can't, Morgan. I wish I could, but I can't."

He frowned, his ingenuous face puzzled. At least, I thought then that it was puzzlement.

"Why not, Ann? I'll meet you at the airport. We can have a wonderful week. We could travel together but if we did I wouldn't get to go."

Deflected for a moment, I asked, "Why not?"

He looked cautiously around but there was nothing near the wall but a grove of scattered olive trees. A hundred yards distant, a cream-colored villa with shuttered windows basked in the warm sunlight.

Even so, his voice dropped to a whisper. "It's really a neat deal. I can't tell you a whole lot about it but I get a free trip and some expense money and all I have to do is deliver a message. I mean, it's really a slick deal!"

I frowned. "Is it something illegal, Morgan?"

He shook his head vigorously. "No, that's the neatest part of all. I'm getting a lot of gold stars from Uncle Sam and they might come in handy some day!"

"Uncle Sam?"

He bent close and his beard touched my cheek and the warmth of his breath stroked my skin. "The CIA. They go in big for messengers. You know, they think the spooks on the other side might rob the mail train if they dropped a letter in the posta. And that means meaty jobs for guys like me. Who thinks anything about an art student taking a trip to Athens? I'll tell you, Ann, it's the only way I'd get to see any place besides Florence. My scholarship won't stretch to an extra pencil case much less trips to Athens."

"That's great, Morgan."

"So you see why we can't travel together. I mean, sometimes they have me use a different passport and things like that. But we could meet in the Hellenikon airport. Come on, Ann."

"Morgan, what kind of scholarship do you think I have?" I asked sharply. "With the increases in the cost of living, my money just barely makes the month. I won't be able to go anywhere all year."

He frowned. "I hadn't thought about that, Ann. Hey, it will be terrible if you have to go home next year and you've never been to Athens or Rome!"

The seed was planted and its roots flourished in envy-rich soil as the week passed and Morgan was not there. I thought of him all the long days and everything combined to bring Athens to mind. I went to a suspense movie and the climactic scene was of a chase through the Parthenon. In lectures that week, Professor Antonini showed slides of the Parthenon's frieze and called it the glory of Athens. Judith bought a box of baklava and insisted upon sharing it. Gerhardt described his walking tour of the Peloponnesus the year before.

Morgan came back, full of excitement over Athens. He brought me pictures and a booklet from the Benaki Museum. The next week, we packed a picnic lunch, bread and cheese and a bottle of Chianti, and rode his cycle out to the Roman baths at Fiesole. Pledging me to secrecy, he said he would be off to Paris in two days. Flinging his arms wide, he exulted, "And all I have to do is take a book to a shop along the Seine and put the book down on top of a barrel at the back of the room. It's beautiful."

Paris.

He brought me back a portfolio of Manet's paintings.

Athens and Paris and all he had to do was a little delivery work.

I made my first trip to Athens five days later. He hadn't

had to urge me. He had called, his voice crackling with excitement, and asked me to meet him in front of the Santa Maria Novella. We sat on a stone bench across the street from that most beautiful of façades and he said eagerly, "I can swing it for you to make some trips, Ann. I told the man I've been working for all about you. He did some checking and made sure you hadn't breathed a word about the trips I've made. He thinks you can do just fine." Morgan leaned close to me. "In fact, there's a letter he wants you to take to Athens."

I went to Athens. It seemed fantastic to have a round trip plane ticket and fifty dollars for expenses. All I had to do was surreptitiously stick an envelope to the bottom side of a table in a small cafe near Constitution Square.

The next week the days turned cooler and clouds often banked high in the Florentine sky. I made a flight to Rome, spent the night, then flew on to Paris. Two letters to deliver.

From the vantage point of knowledge, it is easy to be appalled at such naïveté. But at that moment, Ann Severin was not long from the orphanage and was little schooled in duplicity.

She was to learn.

# X

The telephone rang, wrenching me out of the past. It was as shocking as a blow.

I gripped the chair arms and stared at the telephone on Paul's desk.

It rang again and the sound was as sharp and wrong as shattering glass.

My eyes swung to the clock above the door to the secretary's office. Quarter to two. In the morning.

It rang again.

I pushed up from the leather chair, walked to Paul's desk, and stared down at the telephone.

It rang again.

I looked at the little electric clock on Paul's desk. The second hand was sliding around. Now it was fourteen minutes before two.

And the phone rang again.

No one would call a professor's office at this hour. No one.

A wrong number?

I swallowed and watched the phone as if it were alive and evil.

It rang and rang and rang.

A wrong number would not ring so long.

I knew who called. I reached down and touched the receiver. I slid my fingers around it.

It rang again.

Tormented by the shrill, demanding peal, I wanted to pick

it up and make the ringing stop. My fingers were hard against the smooth, black handset. The impulse was traveling from my brain to the nerve ends when I said aloud, harshly, "No."

I opened my fingers and yanked my hand away from the receiver.

No. I wouldn't dance to his tune. I would give him no least advantage. It would be to his score if I answered that telephone.

If I didn't answer, he couldn't be certain I was here. It was the Mercedes, of course, parked in the lot below, which had betrayed me. Still, if I didn't answer, he couldn't be sure.

The bell rang and rang and rang. I wondered at him. I wondered where he stood, telephone in hand, and what he felt, listening to that continuing peal. Had he been to my house, hunting me? Why had he come to Felson Hall?

No. I wouldn't answer that telephone, but the fact that it had rung was a reminder, if I needed one, that the hunt wasn't over.

Fear washed over me again as it had in the car when I'd hurried away from the airport. Fear is insidious. It overwhelms without warning and turns the back of your throat brackish and pushes the air out of your lungs. I stood by Paul's desk and I was terribly, terribly afraid.

Somebody out there wanted to kill me. Somebody wanted Janey Hamilton to die.

I held on to Paul's desk with hands that trembled. The phone rang and rang and rang and each ring was like a blow until I wanted to scream, "Stop it, damn you. Stop it. Leave me alone." It was both a whimper and a plea.

It seemed an eternity before the ringing stopped.

I pulled air into a chest that ached. I must not give way to panic. My only hope was to think — think clearly. I had evened the battle a little. I had a gun. I had put Margaret out

83

of danger. But I was still the quarry, as distinct and traceable as the brightly painted metal duck in the carnival shooting gallery. Somehow I had to force my pursuer into the open, trick him into revealing his identity.

Was there some way I could entice him to a lonely spot and turn the attack against him? Become the hunter?

Perhaps I should have answered the phone. I would ask for a chance to talk to him, promise to meet him and make it a place where. . . .

At first the little noise didn't penetrate my thoughts, didn't mean anything to me. Metal scraped on metal, lightly, delicately.

I still stood by Paul's desk. The noise sounded again and chains rattling in a dungeon could not have been more frightful. Slowly, scarcely daring to breathe, I turned and looked toward the door into Paul's secretary's office. I had locked that door behind me when I first came. Thank God. I heard the tiny, sharp, clicking sounds and knew they came from the other side of the door.

For an instant that seemed to stretch into infinity, I stood absolutely unmoving, watching and listening.

The door handle moved.

I whirled around, stumbling in my frantic haste to reach the end table by the brown leather chair. Grabbing up the Luger, I swung back to face the door. I held the gun with both hands and aimed right at that knob.

I don't know how long I watched that knob, my arms rigid, my heart thudding as if I'd run a mile. I listened harder than I'd ever listened before. Would a key click into that lock? Would the knob rattle, signaling the opening of the door?

Whose face would I see? A friend? A stranger?

I waited, listening to the rain splashing against the windows beyond the red plush drapes and the asthmatic whuff of the old heating system and then, distantly, the rumble of an elevator.

Did someone still stand beyond that door, listening as I was listening? Or was there only the emptiness of the night?

This was my chance. Perhaps the only chance I would ever have. Oh, Janey, have you already waited too long? Hurry, Janey, hurry!

Hurry to die?

But this is what I had hoped for, wasn't it? The pursuer revealed, the table turned? Hurry Janey.

I reached down, yanked up my coat, and slipped it on, switching the gun from hand to hand but always pointing at the door.

Then I crossed the room to stand beside the door. Now came the difficult part, the moment when I would be most vulnerable. I had a sense of power as long as I could watch that knob and aim the Luger at it. But I couldn't hunt the hunter if I stayed in my burrow. Reaching up, I turned off the lights. The darkness was sudden and absolute, the thick, red plush curtains screening out any faint hint of light from outside. Slowly my hand dropped to the handle of the door. Did I dare unlock it, pull it open? Did someone stand there? Could I react in time if anyone did?

I touched the knob. It was slick under my fingers and I knew my hands were clammy with fear.

The unknown is so much worse than the known.

My hand fell away from the knob. I couldn't do it. I could not open that door. For a moment, I stayed pressed against the door in utter misery, then, abruptly, desperately, I pushed away and began to move as quickly as I dared through the utter darkness toward the filing room. I walked with my hands outstretched, but I knew Paul's office as well as our own living room. I circled past the divan, avoided the floor lamp and, just opposite Paul's desk, I found the door to the filing room. It wasn't locked. I tiptoed through the filing room to the door that opened into the main hall. This, of course, was locked.

I took a deep breath, gripped the Luger in my right hand, and with my left began to edge open the door to the hall. I opened it wide enough for me to slip out into the hall, and I did it all in one swift movement because I knew if I hesitated I would never again be able to force myself out into the hostile well of blackness that was the hall.

How many times had I walked down that hall? Hundreds of times. On bright spring afternoons, hurrying a little, to urge Paul to slip away and play tennis. On somnolent summer mornings to help rearrange the filing cabinets. On snowy winter days, Margaret's mittened hand in mine, welcoming the steamy warmth, walking briskly to meet husband and father for lunch at the Faculty Club.

I gently closed the door behind me and pressed against the plastered wall. The hall was utterly dark. I stared into the darkness by Paul's door. The great windows at either end of the hall were only slightly gray masses in the darkness of this rainwashed night. I strained to see but I might as well have had velvet pressed against my eyes.

All the many times I had walked that hall meant nothing now. There was no comforting sense of familiarity.

I watched Paul's office door for one minute, then another, and gradually concluded that I was alone in the wide hall. I heard no faintest rustle, no lightest stirring of breath, nothing. Cautiously I began to move toward the central stairway. I had waited too long. The hunter had passed this way but he was gone.

If I hurried. . . .

I started down the stairs. I paused to listen at the second-floor landing, then began the next flight, moving like a pad-footed shadow ever closer to the ground floor. Near the bottom of the steps, I stopped to listen. I could hear the gentle splash of the tiled fountain in the main lobby — and the click of shoes as someone walked down the south hall.

I finished the last few steps and began to run softly toward the south hall. I held the Luger out before me, releasing the safety catch with a suddenly moist finger, and knew the truth that possession of a gun changes its bearer. There was intent and deadly purpose in the way I moved.

I reached the south wing and now I could clearly hear footsteps far ahead. Quiet unhurried footsteps. I paused to peer down the hall, and was for the first time uncertain. Whoever walked down the south hall made no effort to hide, no attempt at stealth. Then I began to run again. Why should he be quiet? He could not know I was stalking him.

I moved faster, shortening the space between us. When I heard the fire exit clank open and saw for an instant the lighter darkness of the night, I ran full out, my flats slapping against the marble floor. I reached the exit, pushed through it, and stopped on the concrete step just outside.

I saw him twenty yards away, a man striding down the sidewalk toward the street. He wore dark slacks, a bulky peacoat, and a round knit cap. He was hurrying, his head bent against the rain.

I raised my arm and aimed at the back of that moving figure. I knew I had very little time in which to shoot. I had no idea of the extent of a Luger's range, no idea really whether I could hit a moving target at any distance, and he was moving farther away every second.

I held the gun steady and began to press against the trigger.

The man moved so confidently, so easily, so completely

unaware of danger and death.

Slowly I let the gun swing down.

It might not be him. It might not be the hunter.

You fool, my mind argued, hurry, hurry, shoot him before he gets away, shoot him now.

He was almost to the street.

I stood, the gun heavy in my hand, and knew I couldn't press the trigger. Not this way. I had to be certain. If I knew he was my quarry I would have no pity, no least hesitation because only one of us was going to survive our fated encounter. But I must know absolutely, without possibility of doubt.

He was gone now, lost in the shadows of the evergreens.

I stood on the concrete step, tired, wet, and caught up in a feeling of unreality. Could I, Janey Hamilton, actually be standing in the rain outside Felson Hall at two in the morning with a gun in my hand and murder in my heart?

It was the sound of a car approaching that shook me out of my daze and gave energy and impetus to an exhausted body. Who else might be on the campus at this hour? There was no guessing. It might be late-night revelers finally heading home. It might be the campus police.

I jammed the Luger into my coat pocket and hurried across the sidewalk into the shadows. I felt close to defeat. I was caught up in a nightmare of fatigue and fear and nothing I did seemed to help. Wasn't I an absurd figure, stealing into a professor's house to steal a gun, stalking footsteps down a darkened hall only to let my suspect go? It is devastating to see oneself as absurd. I yanked the gun back out of my pocket and raised my hand to fling it away. I had had my chance and now it was gone. Margaret was unlucky in her mother, unlucky indeed. I had been so close to discovering my enemy, so close. . . .

I stood very still, my arm uplifted, as the sudden realization burst into my mind as bright as white-hot flame. Yes, I was close, very close, yes, indeed. The stalker wasn't so smart, after all. He wasn't so very damn smart, was he?

I shoved the gun back into my coat pocket. I wasn't defeated yet, after all.

Only members of the department and senior clerical workers had keys to Felson Hall. Since the days of student unrest and the highly embarrassing incident several years earlier when a group of activists broke into the graduate college and stole pounds of records, every building on the campus had new and highly sophisticated locks. Not only did the key have to be perfect, indentation for indentation, to turn the lock, but each key carried an invisible legend that activated an electric impulse that made it possible for the key to work at all. So it wouldn't help to make an impression of a key and have a copy made because the copy would lack the proper electronic stimulus.

Each professor had four keys to Felson Hall, one to the building proper, one to his own office, one to the library, and one to the main secretary's office. That was why my pursuer hadn't been able to open Paul's door. The office keys were not interchangeable.

But he had the right keys to get into Felson Hall and open the secretary's door, which meant he was either a faculty member, a secretary, or a nightwatchman. I didn't have too much difficulty figuring out which.

I no longer felt tired. I had narrowed my suspect down to one of Paul's department. And I felt sure I could narrow it still further. It almost had to be a new faculty member. It didn't make sense that it would be someone who had been here for several years. Why wait? So I had a starting point — new members of the department.

What I needed now was to make a list of all the new men

and to learn something about them, see if I could tie them to Florence. I turned and moved back toward Felson Hall. The personnel files in Paul's office would be the answer.

I should be safe enough in the building now since the hunter had passed by there earlier. I was circling around the building, heading back toward the side door, when I saw a campus police car slide to a stop near the front entrance. Two policemen got out and headed toward the front door, swinging their flashlights back and forth on either side of the walk, darting the light beneath the evergreens, raising the beams to flash along the first-floor windows.

I slipped behind an oak tree to watch. Were they making a regular check? Or was this something special? I wondered suddenly if my pursuer could have called them, reporting a prowler near the building. Was he stubbornly sure that I must be somewhere about since the Mercedes was parked in the lot? Did he hope to flush me from hiding in this way? After all, even the wife of the department chairman would have a little difficulty explaining her presence at two in the morning.

I turned and hurried behind a hedge and again felt harried and badgered. Everywhere I turned, something blocked me. Every idea I had was forestalled. I had hoped to spend the night safely in Paul's office, leaving early, before anyone arrived. Now I was once again forced out into the night. And there was no place to go.

One of the policemen turned and was coming to this side of the building. I began to run, softly but quickly, toward the wooded area that bounded this side of the campus. I skirted past the parking lot. I knew better than to approach the Mercedes. I didn't dare retrieve it until day came and the campus surged with people. People. I would be safe when there were people everywhere. All I had to do was find shelter for the rest of the night, then, in the morning, I would go back to Paul's office and study the files. I would tell Nancy, Paul's secretary, that I needed some information on our new faculty members for the monthly department newsletter that I helped put together.

Once I reached the trees, I felt safe from the flickering flashlights of the campus policemen, but it was a nightmarish walk. I slipped on rain-slick leaves and struggled through mud. Low branches slapped at me, snagging my coat. I was so grateful to reach the street on the other side of the trees that I scarcely minded the steady rainfall.

It was a long walk, ten blocks, and the rain never stopped. It was just strong enough to soak me thoroughly.

It was the oddest walk I ever made. No one stirred. It was still too early for the paper boys. Only rarely did light gleam from a house. Dogs did bark. Fortunately, dog owners never seem to take the barking of their dogs seriously. One block before Franklin Drive, I turned down the street and walked to the fourth driveway, then moved from one shadow to another alongside the house.

I did not like this at all. I felt alien, an intruder in the night. It seemed to take forever to reach the back yard, and then loud, friendly woofs split the silence.

"Shh. Here, Sammy, here. Shh," I whispered as the Millers' playful collie danced close to me. I knelt to pet her wet fur, and spoke softly to her as she wriggled happily and barked again. She finally quieted down, accepting the presence of her back yard neighbor, and followed me across the thick, wet grass of her own yard.

At the very back of the Millers' lot, a huge oak reared more than one hundred and fifty feet into the sky. Midway up, still well hidden by autumn leaves, was a super tree house. Once, to my horror, I'd heard Margaret's voice calling from somewhere above me and I'd looked up from weeding the back flowerbed to see her tiny figure at that incredible height.

Somehow I had climbed up and brought her down, and told her that she must never go up that tree again, at least not until she was big like Alan and Jimmy Miller (thirteen and twelve, respectively). Once up in the tree house, though terrified that small hands might lose their grip and small feet slip, I'd been impressed by the sturdiness of the tree house — and secretly thrilled by its remoteness.

It was a much tougher climb this night. The nailed-in slats that formed the ladder were wet and slick. My heavy coat, soggy with rainwater, pulled against me. The Luger banged against my leg. But with one hand over another, one foot up and then another, I climbed to Jimmy and Alan's tree house, and never did a wrecked mariner appreciate shelter more than I appreciated the rough wooden floor of that tree house and the stack of old blankets in the corner. I rolled up in the blankets and finally I was warm again. I lay on the uneven wooden floor and listened to the rain that fell so softly and steadily and endlessly. I listened and remembered another rain that seemed as though it would never end.

# XI

When All Soul's Day dawned, Tuesday, November 1, 1966, no one knew what the week would hold. No one, certainly, had any inkling that the rains were only beginning.

Morgan flew out of Florence on Wednesday. He was supposed to return on Friday. That would have given him ample time to deliver the package and instructions to me. I had always dealt with Morgan. His boss, the "spook," had never met with me. All instruction, tickets, monies, and messages came to me through Morgan.

But the rain continued to fall. Thursday night the storm worsened. Thick, heavy, solid sheets of rain fell all night Thursday, all day Friday, and into Friday night. Before the skies cleared, Florence was ravaged. The placid golden Arno was transformed into an ugly, raging torrent, tearing gaping holes in the Ponte Vecchio, washing away buildings, pouring tons of oily, sludge-laden water over its banks and into the streets.

One hundred and thirteen dead. Six thousand shops demolished. Nine thousand cars wrecked.

The Church of Santa Croce was under twenty feet of water. Six feet of water covered the floor of the Duomo. At the Baptistry, five panels of Ghiberti's bronze doors, the Gates of Paradise, were wrenched away. The National Library was a disaster. The lobby of the Uffizi Gallery was awash.

No electricity, gas, or telephones.

As the waters receded, students waded through the cold waters, clambered up muddy steps, to help, wherever they could as best they could.

At the National Library thousands and thousands of irreplaceable books were caked with mud and oozing oil. I was one of dozens in hip boots sloshing through muddy, water-covered corridors, carrying the books upstairs to spread them carefully open and start the drying out.

I was going downstairs (my eightieth trip that day? nintieth?) when I heard my name called. Softly.

"Ann. Ann Severin."

I looked down the stairs. In the dimness of the hall I saw a man in a trench coat, a hat pulled low over his face. "Someone wants you outside." Then he turned and was gone.

I didn't move. I was tired, very tired. I had worked, awkward in hip boots, since early that morning, wading through the watery corridors, carrying one armload of books after another. I was so tired that it was difficult to think. Who could want to see me? Whoever it was, why didn't they come inside? There was at least some makeshift lighting inside. Irritated, I began to walk down the stairs, moving carefully on the still mud-slick steps. I almost ignored the summons. Every worker was needed to save the books, and the work had to be done immediately.

Whatever it was, it could wait.

I reached the muddy watery hall and, slowly, I turned toward the main doors. Was it the prodding of manners and custom not to ignore a call? Was it curiosity? Was it in hope that Morgan waited without?

Once outside the doors, I hesitated at the top of the steps. It was already dark, a cold, damp dark. The smell of the river was everywhere. The streetlamps weren't working yet so I stood in darkness. I moved slowly down the steps, peering

94

into the night. Suddenly a flashlight beam swept across my face. My eyes shut against the bright glare.

"Over here," came the whispered call.

I squinted. The flashlight beam slid down the steps. Someone stood at the bottom of the steps, holding the flashlight, and I knew it wasn't Morgan. It was the man who had called to me inside the library.

My mind was too tired to puzzle it out. Why should he say that someone wanted me outside if it were he who did?

"Hurry."

Numbly I moved down the stairs, the hip boots a hindrance on every step.

"Morgan sent me," he said, and again his voice was a husky whisper.

"Where is Morgan?"

"In Amsterdam. He hasn't been able to get back because of the flood. Flights will begin leaving Florence tonight, however, and there is a job for you."

I stared at the figure, indistinct behind the light of the flashlight, and began to shake my head. "I can't. I've got to help at the library. They need every. . . ."

"They'll need help for weeks! This other job comes first. It's very important. There's no way of describing how important it is. Morgan was scheduled to have told you about it on Friday, but he couldn't get back to Florence."

His rapid whispers revealed more than he knew. His claim that he came for Morgan was false. I realized that at once. This, obviously, was Morgan's boss, the "spook" who ordered and paid.

I wanted desperately to stay and help salvage the books. The library staff needed every hand. I knew that. But I also felt an obligation — a debt, if you will — to this dimly seen stranger. After all, he had paid my way to Athens and Rome and Paris. And, deep down, I welcomed that extra money. Rarely had I had any money to call my own, to do with as I alone wished.

So a sense of obligation, a dash of cupidity, and the course of my life — and the lives of so many others — was to change, abruptly and irrevocably.

"Will I be gone long?"

"No, it's a short trip this time. Very short."

Someone walked out the doors of the National Library just then. The flashlight beam snapped off. He gripped my elbow.

"Let's walk down the street."

Again his voice was a murmur in the night. He moved darkly beside me, only a warmth, a bulky hat and coat, his face a pale oval in the darkness.

He held my elbow tightly, pushing me almost a half pace ahead of him down the muddy, debris-strewn sidewalk.

We were in sight of the emergency lights hanging at the Palazzo Vecchio, where food and bedding was being distributed to those who had lost everything in the flood, when he pulled me into the deeper shadows of an alley and spoke rapidly and insistently in his whispering voice.

"You must listen closely. At the corner of Castellani and deNeri there is parked a gray Fiat. It is locked. Take these keys and. . . ."

I listened closely. Without giving me a chance to interrupt, he repeated the directions, then whispered sharply, "You must be at the Peretola airport within the hour."

And he turned and walked swiftly away, back toward the library. I stared after him and almost called out, then my hand closed against the crumpled wad of lire in my pocket. It looked to be quite a bit of money. I pulled out the lire and weighed it in my hand, then, when I looked up again, he was gone in the darkness and it was too late to call him back. Forever too late.

I pulled my coat closer around me and began the weary trudge back toward the library. I couldn't leave without giving someone else the hip boots to use. But I soothed my pang of conscience. I would be back in plenty of time to help with the clean up. As the man had said, it was a short trip, a flight to Naples. I would be gone only the one night. And it was such a simple job, really. In fact, my part would be completed before the plane even left the Florence airport.

It cut into the time I had to go back to the library, but I knew the boots were needed. Once I had returned them, I hurried out into the dark night, wishing I had a flashlight of my own. But I made it finally, scrambling over humps of debris and struggling to keep my footing on the mud-coated pavement. It was only three blocks to the corner where the car was parked, but it took me twenty minutes to get there. The Fiat was parked as he had promised. I unlocked it, slipped into the driver's seat and reached up to the sun visor, as I had been instructed, and found another key taped there. Turning on the interior light, I saw the numbers impressed in the metal. It was the key for Locker 45. The attaché case I was to carry onto the flight would be waiting in the locker.

I drove as quickly as I dared down the dark streets. Twice I had to stop and back around a corner and seek another route, my way blocked by flood damage, a crumpled car, tangled lampposts, fallen masonry. When I reached the house I parked half up on the curb, though it was forbidden, ran up the front steps, and pushed in the heavy wooden door.

My room was at the very top and front of the house. I was starting up the narrow steps when Mrs. Giovanetti's door opened and in the fitful light of a candle I saw her inquiring face, a plump face creased with good-natured lines. Tonight it was pale and worried. Her questions rolled out in a quick spatter of Italian, so quick that I could catch only a word here and there. She saw my distress and asked in English, "Is it so bad? Is it so bad as they say on my little transistor radio? That so many have died and so much is lost? At the library, how is it at the library?"

I tried to tell her what I had seen and heard in the stricken, water-weighted city. All the while, I knew the time was fleeting. I must not miss that plane.

"The emergency food, can you help me get some, Ann? Do you know. . . ."

"Yes, yes, Signora Giovanetti, but please, not tonight. I must hurry. I must go."

The idea of hurry was so odd, so out of context, that she stared at me, sure that she had misunderstood, that the English she spoke so well had deceived her.

Then her round, dark face spread with an understanding smile. "Ah yes, they need for you to return to the library to help more? That is it, yes?"

The minutes were running out. Suddenly I felt a frantic need of haste, but how could I tell Mrs. Giovanetti that I was not going to help, that I was leaving town?

And so, another little lie. Later I was to regret that lie, regret it bitterly.

"I have to fly to Naples tonight, signora. It is to deliver some papers for a professor. It is very important. But I will fly back tonight and then I will go back to the library and help. Now I must hurry, I really must. The airplane leaves at eight-thirty and I am almost late now. I must hurry."

"Oh yes, of course. I will help you. Quick, quick, up the steps. I will lead the way with my candle. Quick we go."

She bustled up the steep wooden steps, her square heels

clicking sharply against the bare treads. I hesitated, remembering how the man had insisted, urgently, that I carry only my own passport and not the extra that had been provided for the trip to Paris. And that extra passport was in the false bottom of the purse I was carrying! I couldn't take it out with Mrs. Giovanetti watching!

Then, impatient with myself, I hurried up the steps after her. What difference did it make if I took it along? I would just leave it in its hiding place. What could it possibly hurt if I had it with me? I wasn't even going to cross a frontier.

So I didn't worry any more about it. I was tired, of course. I had had very little sleep since the flood and I had worked, and worked hard, since before dawn at the National Library. So I dismissed the man's direct specific order that I place the extra passport beneath the mattress of my bed.

Why didn't I wonder at that order? Why didn't I think?

The minutes were speeding, as time will when you have too little of it. I slipped out of my cold, wet slacks and sweater, and pulled on a warm brown pants suit, as I thought I might have to go all night without sleep and I wanted to be as comfortable as possible. Mrs. Giovanetti hung up the wet and draggled slacks and clucked about, helping, and the extra passport stayed beneath its false bottom. I grabbed up a scarf and wrapped it about my head, and I was ready.

She called after me as I left, "Have a good flight, Ann, a good flight."

The airport lights were in order so I didn't have any trouble parking the Fiat. Again following specific instructions, I tucked the keys above the visor, then locked the car. In my hand I clutched the key to the locker where I would find the attaché case.

The brown leather case was there. I was startled at its weight when I pulled it out of the locker. I was also shocked and more than a little offended at the small, neat padlock that hung, locked, through the hasp. Did they think I would nose into their damned case? Good grief, I could care less what they put in the stupid thing.

I walked quickly, only five minutes before eight now, to the ticket counter.

"I am Ann Severin. You are holding a ticket for me."

Once again, despite my exhaustion and the flicker of guilt from leaving when every hand was needed, I felt that indefinable lift, that surge of spirit that marks the beginning of a journey.

"Ah yes, Miss Severin, here it is, and please if you will hurry. The plane is loading now at Gate-3."

"Thanks. Prego." I did hurry, and I found the weight of the attaché case a burden. This was, of course, long before the days of grim searches at loading gates and painstaking checks of hand luggage. No one cared that I had an attaché case in hand. No one noticed.

I showed my ticket and followed a line of travelers. Someone ahead carried a crying baby. Poor baby, I thought. I couldn't know what an unlucky baby that was.

Directly in front of me marched a young family, papa, mama, and five boys. As we climbed up the steps and into the plane, we found it full of movement, the stowing of bags and taking off of coats.

I walked down the aisle and slipped into a seat over the wing, as I had been instructed. I shoved the attaché case beneath the seat, then sat back and watched the people filing down the aisle. The plane was almost full now. I reached forward and pulled out a magazine, a European edition of *Time*. The PA system crackled and a moment later came announcements in Italian, English, German, and French.

"We regret to inform you that this flight will be delayed

half an hour. Passengers may alight and wait in the lounge until the flight is called. Thank you for your patience."

Gradually the plane emptied. Some passengers grumbled. One older lady plucked at her daughter's arm and her plaintive questions reflected a basic fear of flying. A Florentine businessman shrugged and invited his friend to the bar for a drink.

I was impatient. The longer before the plane left, the longer it would be until I could return. I knew, of course, that I wasn't indispensable or terribly important to the rescue efforts, but every willing pair of hands could be of some help. And it was such important help, to salvage the treasures of the ages.

The passengers straggled across the concrete and through the gate. Inside, some headed directly for the bar and restaurants. Others meekly arranged themselves in the plastic-backed chairs and began to wait. I paced up and down before the windows, peering out into the night, wondering how long it would be. Then I stopped in midstride, stopped and looked with narrowed eyes at the long, sleek line of the plane.

The man had instructed me so clearly, "Put the case beneath your seat," he had said. "That is all you have to do. Absolutely all. Your responsibility is then fulfilled. Place the case. Do not touch it again. Someone else will retrieve it in Naples. All you have to do is leave the plane in Naples without a backward glance. Is that clear?"

Clear as clear as clear. I turned and hurried away from the lounge, wishing that I had not locked up the Fiat with its keys inside as I had been told to do. It would have been a good deal easier to get into town with the car, but I would manage. I would get a taxi. After all, I had that wad of lire in my pocket.

How simple it was. If all I had to do was put the stupid

locked case beneath the seat, well, I had done it. Why should I fly to Naples? Someone else, probably a stewardess, would pick up the case at the end of the flight.

I went directly to the National Library. I didn't give that plane another thought. Not one single thought. I carried books and gently spread them out to dry as long as I could slosh one foot in front of the other. My brown pants suit would never be the same. But what did it matter? It was nearing dawn when I curled up in a rough woolen blanket in a back hall with several other girls who had been helping and I was asleep almost instantly even though the marble floor was cold and hard.

The voices woke me, the low, shocked voices a few feet away.

"How dreadful! Are you sure?"'

"Yes, I heard it on my transistor. The plane exploded over the Bay of Naples. A yacht and a fishing boat saw it so there's no mistake about it. It was an explosion right in the middle of the plane. They're almost sure it had to be a bomb."

"God."

"Yeah, pretty lousy, all right, on top of everything else. They haven't released the passenger list yet but the announcer said it was rumored that Professor Antonini was on board."

I was struggling to my feet now. I reached out and gripped the arm of the boy who was speaking.

"What plane?" I demanded. "What plane?"

He stared at me, then said slowly, "Flight 103. From Florence to Naples."

I didn't say anything. I couldn't.

"I'm sorry," he said after a moment. "Did someone you. . . . That is, the casualty list hasn't been made public yet. So maybe. . . ." His voice trailed off.

"A bomb," I said in a hard, thin voice. "They think it was a bomb?"

He nodded unhappily. "Yes. From what they've pieced together, it looks like the plane blew up right between the wings. It exploded, there was a flash of flame, then it all dived down into the water."

"Did anybody . . . ?" I couldn't finish. I knew the answer even before he reluctantly shook his head.

# XII

White-faced, my hands trembling, I held the flimsy newspaper and stared at the names and saw my own midway down the list.

Severin, Ann, 21, American.

Fifty-four dead. By my hand.

I crumpled the newspaper and walked to a park, and huddled on a stone bench, a shaken, lost being. I had put the case beneath the seat, the very seat where now they said the explosion had originated.

*But I didn't know it,* I wept within, *dear God, I didn't know it, I didn't.* Pushing up from the bench, I ran toward the river and stared into the ugly, swollen, brown waters. I don't know how long I leaned against the parapet and wept for the baby on that airplane and for his mother and for the stocky businessman with the sprinkle of silver in his crisp black hair. And for myself.

It was late afternoon when I stumbled the long muddy way back toward Mrs. Giovanetti's. I don't know what I intended. To go to the police? But why should they believe me? Why should they even listen to my tale of "the man," the man I had so briefly and so indistinctly seen on the steps of the National Library? Wasn't this just another lie, they would say, such as when I told Mrs. Giovanetti I was carrying papers for a professor?

If Morgan were only here. . . . When Morgan got back to Florence, he could confirm my story about the man and, even if Morgan and I had broken some rules, some laws, in working for the man, surely we could convince the authorities that we had been innocent messengers.

I felt a great sense of relief. Morgan would help me when he came back. It was then, for the first time, that the frightful thought occurred to me that Morgan might have connived to deceive me. *No,* my heart cried, *no!* Morgan was as much a dupe of the man as I had been. Oh, when would Morgan be back from Amsterdam?

I was at the narrow block that led to Mrs. Giovanetti's house — and there was a police car parked in front of the house. Slowly I looked up and, yes, there at the third floor I could see a man standing by the window in my room.

Whirling around, I hurried back the way I had come.

So the police were there. What would they think if I were to walk in, alive, unharmed? As I walked away from the house I pulled a scarf from my pocket, wrapped it around my head, and hunched down into my coat collar. If anyone saw me, recognized me. . . .

At that moment the realization came to me that it would be very dangerous indeed if anyone recognized me. In fact, it might be quite fatal. Because the man, that dimly seen soft-spoken man, had intended that I should die in that flaming crash. I was to have been the instrument of death for fifty-five, not fifty-four. Only I had not reboarded the flight.

If the man saw me, he must silence me.

Then I began to run, realizing that I could not wait for Morgan. I was in mortal danger every second that I stayed in Florence. I might even bring danger to Morgan if I waited for him. So I began to run, never really hoping, only fearing. Moving swiftly, jerkily as a frightened animal will, unable to see ahead, unable to know the outcome, but always trying.

I had no plan, nothing to direct me from this clump of brush to that, only the instinct to flee. The long trail began very simply. I walked to the bus station and took a second-class bus to Rome. Only when I reached Rome did I begin to think what I might try next.

I was afraid to use the name Ann Severin. I thought then of that extra passport, the passport I had been so strictly instructed to hide beneath my mattress. Had that been planned too? Of course, of course. If the Florentine police had any doubts about the guilt of passenger Severin, they should be quelled by the discovery of a false passport.

But how would the shadowy man ever know whether that passport had been found? He might, of course, have an informant among the police. Still, if it wasn't found, wouldn't he just assume that I had taken it with me and that it was now lost for all time?

So I should be able to use it with safety for at least a while.

It was this thought that prodded me to keep on going, once I made it to Rome. I took a bus to the airport. Dawn was breaking by the time I arrived. I freshened up in a restroom and, furtively, destroyed Ann Severin's passport and papers. Then I counted my money, that crumpled wad of lire. I had enough, just enough, to buy a ticket on an Air India flight going to Frankfurt, London, and New York.

No one questioned me. No one stopped me. The passport occasioned no notice at all. But the inspector at Customs in New York was suspicious of me. This was before the day of great hordes of unwashed, sandaled and bearded students with little or no luggage.

"You don't have any luggage? Not a single case?" the inspector demanded, and his pale gray eyes were sharp and inquisitive.

I shook my head stupidly. I had been without sleep for a long, long time. I blinked and tried to pull my mind together.

"I had a suitcase."

I shrugged. "It was stolen in Rome. I had everything in it. But it doesn't matter too much. I'm on my way home."

"And where do you live?"

I looked at him blankly and then, with a supreme effort, remembered the town listed in the passport. "Madison. Madison, Wisconsin."

He stared at me for a long moment, then shrugged. "Okay," and he stamped my card and I was free to go.

Have you ever been to New York, getting close to broke, running scared and completely unfamiliar with the city? It's not a nice thing. With the time change from Rome to New York, what had begun so many hours ago as a morning flight now ended at eight o'clock as I stumbled out of the airport door and into a bitterly cold November night.

I slept on a bench at the West-Side Airlines Terminal that night. The next morning I walked to a bus terminal and studied the rate schedules. Eeney, meeney, miney, moe, where should I go? I picked St. Louis. That's all I had the money for, a ticket to St. Louis and five dollars left over.

I got off the bus two days later and I didn't know the name of a single person, a single street. I would not have felt more alien in a Turkish village. But I walked out of that bus station as if I knew where I was going. I couldn't afford to attract the attention of the police because in my purse I had five dollars and a fake passport.

It was a cold morning in St. Louis. People moved briskly along the streets, square, solid people, many with the bullish heads and high color of the Germans. They looked prosperous, self-assured, and in a hurry. I imagine I must have looked incredibly scruffy and unkempt.

I stopped midway down the block from the bus station and peered at my reflection in a plate-glass window. I smoothed back my hair and straightened my coat, then moved on down

107

the block to a cafe. At the counter I ordered coffee and a doughnut — and wanted to snatch the plate away from the overweight boy next to me. I wanted his two skinny strips of bacon and small mound of scrambled eggs more than I've ever wanted any food before or since. I ate the doughnut very slowly with great draughts of coffee between bites, but too soon it was gone and my hunger only awakened. The girl behind the counter poured me another cup of coffee and I savored it.

What was I going to do?

Five dollars minus ten cents for the coffee and fifteen for the doughnut, that would leave me four dollars and seventy-five cents, and it was a cold November morning in St. Louis.

It was simple, really. Money. I had to get some money.

Then I saw the card tucked in the corner of the mirror that ran the length of the wall behind the counter.

WAITRESS WANTED: INQUIRE AT CASHIER

I didn't have a social security card. I didn't even have a name. But I had to try.

The cashier, a heavy-faced woman of forty, waited impatiently while I fumbled in my purse. I laid the five-dollar bill on the counter, then asked, "I saw the card that said you needed a waitress. Are you still looking for somebody?"

She looked at me with tired eyes, eyes that had seen more than they ever wanted to see. They didn't find any joy in appraising me.

"You ever been a waitress?"

"Yes." You learn to wait tables in an orphanage.

"References?"

"Not from here. I worked in Dallas last."

"Yeah."

Another customer was behind me now.

108

"Okay, we'll try you. Be here at eleven o'clock. Ask for Gladys."

That was the first of a string of jobs. I would fill out the employee questionnaire. Name, Ann Smith; Age, 21; Hometown, Miami Fla., and then, social security number. I made up a new number with each job and I never stayed long enough for the roof to tumble in. I was in Tulsa at Christmas, then on to Dallas, Ft. Worth, Albuquerque, Needles, and finally Los Angeles.

I worked and dreamed of Morgan. On the street, I would see a familiar hunch of shoulders and, knowing it could not be, I would hurry and catch up — and it never was. I wrote him letters, ten letters, twenty letters, and never mailed one of them. I could never let him know I was safe because I had run too far and too long for the police ever to believe I was guiltless.

So I worked for a while, then moved on. I knew when I got to Los Angeles that I couldn't wander from city to city forever. Somehow I had to become somebody. I had to start living again. Ann Severin was dead, but I was alive — alive and nameless. You can't spring full-blown to life in Los Angeles at age twenty-two like Minerva from the head of Zeus. In a computerized, programmed, ticketed society you have to have credentials. You have to be real. You have to have a birthdate and a hometown and a past. I didn't know how in the world I was going to manage it. How could I be real and make believe at the same time?

It was tougher finding a job in Los Angeles. I looked for three days and didn't find anything except one cafe where I could tell the manager wouldn't be interested in how I would serve the customers. I turned down that offer. For no good reason or ill, I caught the bus that afternoon to Long Beach.

It was a pretty city. Downtown it looked like a midwestern

city with moderately tall buildings and straight, flat streets. I walked all the way down the long main street to the harbor area and found myself in one of those beautiful parks that abound in California, the grass neat and short and brightly green, the hibiscus flaming with color. This particular park was full of old people, some spruce and cheerful, others worn and sunk in their pasts. Some played shuffleboard or checkers or horseshoes. Some sat in dreaming quiet on the green wooden benches. For a while I thought I was the only person there under seventy. Then I saw a girl my own age sitting on the grass beneath a pepper tree. She had springy blond hair tied up in doggy ears and a round, cheerful face, the kind you used to see painted on Dresden dolls. Her wide mouth split in a grin when our eyes met and she spread her hand to indicate that the grass was free, and I should have a seat.

I did. I was hungry to talk to someone. How long had it been now, five months, six, and all I'd said to any living soul was, "Do you want your eggs over easy?" or "Coffee now?" or "Yes, sir, it is a pretty day," and "Thank you very much."

I sat down and that was how I met Janey Torbet.

It's funny. I never did tell Janey anything about Florence and, much as she loved to talk and much as she drew strength from knowing and caring about people, she never asked me.

Only once did she say anything to show that she sensed I was in trouble. It was after I had moved in with her in the room she rented in one of the decayed beach hotels. She had looked at me gravely and said, "Ann, you don't belong here. You ought to go back to wherever you're from."

I had shaken my head slowly and my face must have told her there was no place for me to go. She never said it again, never asked a question, never pried. I loved Janey Torbet. Everyone did. Everyone from nervous, narrow-faced Al who ran the drive-in where we both worked to the raucous, rough gang of boys who skidded their Harley-Davidsons into the lot and ate hamburgers with a great hunger and clustered around Janey with even greater hunger. She wasn't truly pretty. Her face was too round and her features too even, but she had magnificent eyes, wide blue eyes that seemed to shine like the sun shining on bright water. She would fasten those gay, laughing, kind blue eyes on me, or Al, or Terry, the boy with the thick brown curls and huge chest, and each of us would know that we had for an instant, so long as those eyes stared into our own, truly communicated with another human being. It was this trick, which was so beautifully no trick at all, that endeared her to everyone she met. The stalls she served were always full, from six in the evening when we went on duty until two in the morning when the Rodeo Drive-In closed.

It was Janey, of course, who got me that job. That first day in the park, how had she known I was lost and hunting a job and broke and getting scared again? I asked her once and she shrugged and smiled and opened those blue eyes wide and said dreamily, "I just knew. Besides, you looked like we would be friends." It was her honesty that made her so different. There was never any side to Janey.

For the first time since I left Florence, perhaps for the first time ever, I began to relax and to lose that unnatural composure that marks all driven people.

Janey chattered most of the time, light, inconsequential talk, usually about other people, but in the course of it I learned about Janey and her past, her actual, solid, real past. She was from a little town in Oregon, Olivet, population 2,483. Her mother had died of cancer when Janey was a junior in high school. Her father had been killed in a car-truck crash two weeks after her high-school graduation. That was all the family she had — no brothers or sisters or aunts or cousins. Janey had sold the small frame house and taken a bus to Los Angeles where she'd met a boy named Ray. They had planned to marry, but he was killed in Viet Nam four days before he would have been rotated home and eight days before their planned wedding. She had moved to Long Beach then because one part of her life had ended and she had to start another. She loved to play checkers and go to the movies and eat saltwater taffy, and she was always a little apart from everyone, even from Terry, the big young man who kept coming back although she said all she could ever be with anyone now was friends. Terry didn't believe that and I thought too that some day she would turn the corner and put away Ray's picture and make Terry one of those rare beings, a happy man.

I always counted those days as special. It is an almost otherworldly experience to encounter a truly gentle spirit.

It was a Saturday night in August that she didn't come home. After work that night she waved good-bye to me from the back of Terry's cycle and called that she would be in soon. I walked home, I remember. It was a mile from the Rodeo to the little hotel where we lived, the Sea Castle. There is a magic about any city in the quiet hours before dawn. They can be dangerous hours, too, but we had never been afraid in Long Beach. Sailors on leave would usually call out, follow for a moment, but no one persisted. I would never have dared that long walk the first time except that Janey said it was all right and we walked and it was fine.

The moon was full that August night and the air was cool and fresh and smelled of the sea. As I neared our hotel I could hear the distant sound of a piano. We always heard it when we walked. I knew it came from one of the little bars down the street. I knew, too, that I never wanted to go to that bar. To go would destroy the magic of that music, its quality of coming from afar, from the past. I remember the lonely click of my shoes on the sidewalk and the fuzzy shine of the high streetlamps in the moist air and the haunting strains of "In the Still of the Night." I could still hear the piano as I climbed the four narrow flights of stairs to our little room at the back. The window was open and the music drifted in, slow and sad. I kicked off my shoes and made a little pan of cocoa on the tiny stove that nestled in the closet-sized kitchenette. I made enough for two, then poured my share into a yellow mug and curled up on the worn sofa to drink it and rest, and listen without thought, without pain, to the distant notes of the piano.

Then the far-off keys slipped into "Arriverdérci, Roma." Tired, my defenses down, the old longing swept me. Oh, Morgan, we should have had so many happy years together, years full of color and promise and beauty. How could I bear it, never to see you again, never to love you?

I slept finally, the scratchy pillow of the sofa wet with tears.

The policeman came at six-thirty. The sharp knocking battered through my sleep. I struggled up and hurried to the door.

When I opened it and saw a policeman, I thought the long run was ended. I stood, wordless, and waited, wondering hopelessly how they had found me.

The policeman's eyes fell from my face to my blouse and he slowly nodded, then said almost reluctantly, "You work at the Rodeo, right?"

My hand reached up to touch the rough red thread that looped flamboyantly over and around my pocket, forming RODEO in a vivid, curving arc.

"Yes." I stared at him, waking sharply now. I saw the stubble of his grayish beard and his worried blue eyes, straining to see from behind thick-lensed glasses.

"I'm sorry, young lady. I'm afraid I have bad news for you."

I reached out and gripped the door. Was he sorry, I wondered, that he must arrest me?

He was looking down at a little notebook in his hand. "I talked to the manager of the Rodeo, Mr. Alan Romaine. He said yes, he had a blond girl who worked for him. Two blond girls, in fact, and they lived together." The policeman's sad eyes looked into mine, then dropped back to his notes. "Janey Torbet and Ann Smith." He looked at me again and slowly I nodded, slowly and hopelessly.

"I'm sorry, miss," he said slowly. "Your friend must have died instantly. A trailer truck lost its brakes. It threw the motorcycle two hundred feet, killing both riders."

The words rolled like marbles, hard, dancing pellets striking glass, meaningless sounds.

I don't remember that he helped me to the couch but, finally, as the hopeless tears slipped down my face, I felt the warmth of his hand patting my shoulder, and heard his gentle voice.

"I'm sorry, young lady. Tell me, was she your sister?"

I shook my head.

"Well, I'm sorry to have to ask it, but will you come with me now?"

I looked up at him, not understanding.

"We have to have someone identify her. And I'll have to ask you to do that unless you know how I can get in touch with her family."

"She doesn't . . . she didn't have anybody. Her folks are dead."

"Well then, young lady, will you please come and identify her? You see, she didn't have a purse with her. Or, if she did, we didn't find it. All we have is the fact that she's a blond girl who worked at the Rodeo Drive-In. We traced her because of the uniform."

I nodded. Janey never liked to carry a purse. Probably her purse was still tucked in the top of our dresser. Numbly, I pushed up from the divan, crossed to the dresser, opened the top drawer, and there it was, a soft, leather-fringed purse. I picked it up and turned to face the policeman.

"Yes, I'll come if you need me."

It wasn't a long drive, but later, I never liked to think about that drive through the steely grayness of the early morning with its fresh and clean scent of a new day.

At the hospital, he led me to a closed door in the basement. He opened it and walked across the room, and I followed.

She didn't look like the same person at all. It wasn't only the massive injuries. It was the blotting out of that shining spirit by death.

"Is it your roommate?" The words seemed to come from a long way away.

I nodded wordlessly.

"What is her name, please?"

I stared down at that unmoving, never-to-move-again figure. It wasn't Janey there. It was absurd to say that that bloodied, crumpled thing had been Janey.

"I'm sorry, young lady. I know it's hard, but we have to make arrangements. You said she had no family. Who is she?"

I looked at him then.

No family. No family at all.

I looked back again at that lifeless figure, then said slowly, "Her name was Ann Smith. I don't know much about her. We met in a park. . . ."

# XIII

It was a long way in time and space from that narrow room and the forever-stilled figure on the table to a children's hideaway in an old oak tree. I huddled in the blankets and my body began to warm, but nothing could help the core of icy fear within me.

Six years ago in Florence, I had been a good deal younger and it had been easier by far to turn and run than to face the horror of what I had caused, even though innocently. From the wisdom of an older Janey Hamilton, it was easy to say that I should have gone to the police then. Easy to say, but I wondered if perhaps I might still be in an Italian prison had I done so.

But I had not gone to the police. I had run and, I thought, run successfully. When Janey died I took the ultimate gamble and assumed her name. Until this morning I had never doubted the wisdom of that gamble. When the day began I'd been Janey Hamilton, secure in her small world. I was no longer secure, but I was still stubbornly, defiantly, to the death, Janey Hamilton.

To the death. . . . My death or his?

Vengeance. It smacked of other days, of blood feuds and bloody retribution. It must mean that a relative or lover of one of the passengers had traced me, had somehow picked up the trail of Ann Severin.

My eyes ached with fatigue. I could scarcely keep them open but I knew that something didn't ring true.

I rubbed my eyes and blinked them wide. I must think.

What was wrong with that conclusion? The crayoned note and the advertisement in the Personals column and the spray-painted tombstone all implied retribution.

Think, Janey, think. You've remembered now, you've dredged up from deep recesses in your mind the whole memory of Florence, the Florence you've spent five years forgetting.

Slowly, grudgingly, my tired, overstimulated mind worked it out.

A relative or friend of a passenger would never have seen Ann Severin and could in no way have known her features well enough to recognize her years later and half a world distant under a new name and securely ensconced in a new life.

I sat up and clutched the edge of the blanket close to me, and I was wide awake now, wide awake.

Moreover, no one knew Ann Severin had carried a bomb aboard but one person — Morgan's "spook." And perhaps Morgan. (*No,* my heart cried, *not Morgan.*) Yes, I must include Morgan because the man, that long-ago night, had said that Morgan would have given me my instructions if it hadn't been for the flood. (Even if that were true, my heart responded, it would have been instructions given by a Morgan innocent of what the attaché case contained. Morgan loved me! He wouldn't have knowingly let me carry a bomb aboard an airplane.)

Nonetheless, my mind reasoned coldly, both Morgan and his spook would know Ann Severin, no matter how many years had passed. And it would be quite a shock to either, after thinking me dead all this while. (But wouldn't it be a joyous shock to Morgan?)

I rubbed my face nervously. The spook or Morgan. Then I sagged back against the rough wooden walls of the tree house, uncertain again.

If it were one of them, why bother? Why wrap up a murder in fancy dress? Why not just stab me in a dark alley? Why drag up the past, wrap Ann Severin's name onto Janey Hamilton's body?

Because the police would hunt hard for Janey Hamilton's murderer, they would seek him out in all the people she knew at the university. They would question everyone she knew. How convenient to suggest that a grieved relative of a passenger had relentlessly trailed Ann Severin to a final accounting. Perhaps my killer even intended to tuck an explicit note into my dead hand. No doubt the police wouldn't be surprised at anything should the murdered wife of an English professor turn out to be a girl presumably lost in an air crash years ago!

It would certainly turn the eyes of the police away from the campus, far away from the man who had keys to enter Felson Hall.

My pursuer was clever.

Morgan had been clever. But I would recognize Morgan, I had no doubt of that. I would know the line of his jaw, the shape of his head, the bright blue of his eyes anywhere. In heaven or hell, I would recognize Morgan.

My heart gave a glad little leap, then sank again immediately. Because I had not yet met all the new faculty members in Paul's department. I would know them all before the year was out. Paul and I always had an open house over the Christmas holidays and invited everyone in the department. I had met several of the newcomers at the President's Reception. Some of these I had seen again at the art museum on the day I'd led the tours.

None of these could be Morgan. But Morgan could be one of the newcomers I had not met. (The Morgan who had held me and told me my hair was the color of Venetian gold?) Somehow I found it difficult to imagine Morgan catching up a rattlesnake and loosing it to lie in wait for me. Morgan had been . . . Morgan had been fun! And though he might know where you could buy marijuana, he never sold it himself. That, he explained to me once, could land you in jail for a long time. Could Morgan, laughing Morgan, jockey a car close and hard to a Mercedes down a steep, straight hill and hang with it almost to a smash?

I didn't know.

But it had to be Morgan or his spook.

The spook.

I closed my eyes and tried to find a comfortable spot on the slanting boards of the tree house. If it had to be one or the other, I would rather it be Morgan even if it turned all my memories of him to bitterness. I felt I could match wits with Morgan. I was not terrified of Morgan.

There is something about the unknown that paralyzes the soul. I had no measure of Morgan's spook.

Tired as I was, depleted as I was, I tried to remember more clearly that long-ago night in Florence. I had seen him from the top of the stairs and not thought about his height. Anyone seen from above seems shorter. Could I recall his size? Recall any salient fact about him at all?

I remembered when he took my arm and pulled me down the street with him. Where was his shoulder to my head? He was taller than I, of course. But how much taller? I had twisted my head and looked up and seen his hat and the pale oval of his face.

Think, Janey, think.

Five feet ten, perhaps six feet tall.

Oh, that helps a lot, Janey dear. Damnit, think!

Closer to six feet. He had worn a raincoat and not been noticeably fat or thin. A medium man, in fact. I don't think I saw his hair. His face was only a shape in the darkness.

119

Would I know his voice if I heard it again?

Slowly, hopelessly, I shook my head. He had spoken in a whisper. No, his voice wouldn't betray him.

Morgan or the spook.

The spook or Morgan.

I finally plummeted down into sleep. My mind had taken as much as it could bear this long day and night. I slept and dreamed and saw Morgan's smiling face and strained to see a dark figure at the bottom of mud-slick stairs.

# XIV

The wind woke me. The old tree swayed under the force of the harsh winter wind. Branches creaked and leaves flurried. It was much colder. I rolled out of the blankets and struggled stiffly up onto my hands and knees, then looked out the triangular window hole at the back of the tree house.

It was a day for death, for the death of summer, for the bleaching of color and vigor from the earth. I shivered as I looked out at the lowering sky, the wet ground and the wind-whipped trees. I could see the back of our own yard. The rain had beaten down the last of my crysanthemums and drenched the lawn furniture that I had not been home to pull into the garage. I studied the back of my house as if it were an enemy encampment. There was no flicker of movement behind the blank, dark windows, but I didn't succumb to the sudden longing to go home, if only for an instant. No. I might be inept in my own defense, but I wasn't stupid. Again, the thought flickered that the house was so obviously empty. I could shower, put on fresh clothes, face Paul's office staff so much more easily. I was tempted, then, resolutely, I shook my head. It would be foolish to take any chances now. That I had survived to this point seemed an omen that my luck had turned. I felt a surge of confidence. I was the hunter now. I was going to make it!

I stacked the blankets back in the corner of the tree house, then gingerly poked my head out the front opening. The oak was far at the back of the Millers' lot. Two smaller maples and a weeping willow screened the base of the oak from the Millers' house. From the tree-house opening I could see the whole of their back yard. No one was outside, which was scarcely surprising since it was so cold and raw and windy.

Now looked as good a time as any to go down. I felt the full strength of the wind as soon as I swung out and started to climb down. The wind was a fearsome thing thirty feet above ground. It tugged at my coat and strummed the smaller branches. I was cold through my damp coat by the time I reached the ground.

I tried to smooth the wrinkles out of my coat and patted at my hair so that I wouldn't look so disreputable. I hurried up the Millers' drive then, and was glad when I reached the sidewalk without seeing anyone, not even the collie.

The wind pushed against me as I walked and I pulled my coat tight. Once on the campus, I went straight to the Felson Hall parking lot. Plenty of cars surrounded the Mercedes now and I didn't hesitate to go to it. There were always people coming and going on the campus in the mornings. No one would dare to attack me now. I opened the trunk and got my purse, and it was absurd how strengthening it was to know that I would soon have my lipstick and comb in hand. While still hunched over the trunk, after a quick look around, I transferred the Luger from my pocket to my purse, then slammed the trunk and walked briskly to the Union. Inside, I was struck by the lovely smell of bacon and eggs and coffee wafting up from the basement cafeteria. I realized abruptly that I was ravenous. I would eat after I had freshened up.

I went to a little-used restroom on the third floor. After I had washed my face and combed my hair and put on some lipstick, I really didn't look too bad. My blouse was wrinkled, of course, but my double knit slacks scarcely showed the effects of the long night. I looked a little rumpled but not enough to excite any notice.

I did take time out for breakfast, and it was marvelous how restored I felt when I finished. I spoke to several students and professors that I knew. I thought I saw Andrew across the room but I wasn't sure. I did see one of the new members of the department. I had met him at the President's Reception. I remembered his face and thought his name was James. He nodded to me as he passed by my table with his tray. I was raising my coffee cup to my lips but I put it down untasted. Could he be the one? It seemed suddenly colder in the cheerful cafeteria.

Determinedly, I picked up the cup again and took a deep swallow. Don't borrow trouble, Janey, I warned myself. Don't let the fear circle around you again. But the fine edge was off my restoration to human society. I finished in a hurry. The sooner I got to those files, the better.

I felt a little uneasy when I first reached Felson Hall. This was the tiger's lair, this was where he prowled. But once I stepped inside, it seemed just as usual, familiar, ordinary, commonplace. I waved good morning to Thomas, the custodian, then stopped to chat for a moment with Professor Staubaugh, who was so unfailingly gentle and courteous.

"It is such a pleasure to see you this morning, dear child," he said.

Anyone under forty was a "dear child" in his eyes.

"It's been too long since you've had dinner with us, Matthew. I will call you when Paul gets back in town."

"Thank you, my dear. I will look forward to it."

And I felt a sudden pang. He had been widowed last March. We had all rallied round then. But for how long? I would call him. If I survived. Odd to file away plans for a social engagement while involved in a struggle for life.

I saw others I knew on the three flights up to Paul's office.

I felt very safe and secure by the time I reached Nancy's desk.

She was surprised to see me but it never occurred to her to question why I needed to study the personnel folders. She followed me to the door of the file room. "Is there anything I can do to help, Mrs. Hamilton?"

"I don't believe so, Nancy, but thank you. I'll call you if I need a hand."

With that she returned to her desk. I could hear her sporadic typing as I got to work.

I went through the folders carefully and slowly, pulling out those of the new faculty members. I found nine new ones. I carried the folders to a worktable and looked at the names, typed neatly on the tabs, last name first:

Birman, Frederick

Channing, Andrew Elwood

Dubois, Ray Flood

Keith, Harris B.

James, Alan Robert

Maxwell, Theodore S.

Riddell, Daniel David (he of the foolish, prating wife).

Stein, Milton

Wyzanski, Roger J.

The only one I knew with any real sense of familiarity was Andrew. Of the others, some I had met at the President's Reception last Friday. Most of them I had never seen. Nine men, all of whom I would be sure to meet before the end of the school term. Was that what had marked me for death?

I was taking a gamble, of course, that my pursuer was among this small group. But he had to be a member of Paul's department, else how had he managed a key to Felson Hall? Yes, he had to be one of the new men.

Each folder contained much the same material though all differed, of course, in the same manner that one man's cut of clothes differs from another even if taken from the same swath.

Some folders I put aside after only a brief survey. Dr. Birman was a distinguished seventy-two-year-old author and essayist whose own university had been so shortsighted as to insist upon mandatory retirement for all faculty at age seventy. He had spent the previous year as a guest lecturer at the University of London, and was this year gracing our campus.

Harris B. Keith had graduated cum laude from Princeton and was here to work on his master's degree and hold his first teaching apprenticeship. He was twenty-two years old, which meant he'd been sixteen when I'd fled Florence.

Theodore S. Maxwell was an authority on Keats and was confined to a wheelchair from the effects of spinal meningitis.

Those three folders I set aside. Six now to study harder.

First I studied each attached photo. I looked with eyes sharpened by fear and with hard-pressed memory. In none of them did I see Morgan's rollicking spirit. But how well did this sort of photo convey personality? I tried to imagine a serious-faced Morgan without a beard or with glasses or with a heavy face.

No. Morgan was not one of these six men, of that I was sure. My heart smiled. I hadn't wanted it to be Morgan. I still could cherish my memories of him, and cherish them I would. It wasn't that I did not love Paul, for I did, wholly, solidly, enduringly, and I was fighting now for that love, but it did no harm for me to remember those golden-toned days in Florence when I was young and beautiful and in love for the very first time. My heart sang at the certainty that none of these men could be Morgan.

Could any of these six men be that dimly seen, dimly remembered figure at the base of the library steps?

I began with Andrew's folder. His dark and handsome face

wore a half smile in the photo, his sensuous mouth curved as if he knew many secrets (he had tried to kiss me last night . . . kiss and kill?). He was thirty-three years old, a bachelor, an authority on E. M. Forster. Where had he been in 1966? Ah, Munich. I thought about that for a long moment. Munich. Not far, really, from Florence. Morgan's spook could have lived in another European city. I knew nothing about him. Munich. Yes, it could be Andrew. (Andrew had a superb overhead smash.) I put Andrew's file in a separate pile, the pile of possible pursuers.

Next came Dubois, Ray Flood. A novelist (*Spring Again*, *Floodtide*, *Running Bright*), forty-three years old, twice divorced. I looked at his picture and remembered him from the President's Reception. His face revealed a good deal more than he would have liked, the fashionably long and thick hair with its artful streak of white, the bulging eyes with the telltale pouches beneath, the dark unholy face, soft and overripe as a rotting plum. In 1966? Writing in Majorca. That kind of author. Yes, it could be. It could very well be. I placed his file atop Andrew's.

James, Alan Robert. I flipped open the folder's cover and stared down at the handsome, boyish face in the photo. It was he I had seen in the cafeteria this morning — and his face had not been nearly so charming as this one. His picture glowed with WASP confidence. The resumé had all the right touches, the right schools, the right scholarships, the right awards. Alan James had done everything right. He was married to a Phi Beta Kappa and had two children. A boy and a girl, of course. (Why had he breakfasted at the Union? A lazy wife? A late night?) He was an all-American from Rutgers and had spent four years in the navy. An officer and a gentleman. I looked at that confident, satisfied face and I had a hard time seeing a spook. And certainly not the kind of spook who so

126

artfully planned the disintegration of an airplane and everyone aboard it. I ran down the list of appointments and for an instant my breath caught in my throat — 1966, advanced studies at the University of Milan. I looked at the picture with new eyes. Was it really so bland?

I added James's folder to my growing stack of possibilities.

Riddell, Daniel David. Undergraduate and graduate degrees from the University of Nebraska. He was thirty. A bit young to qualify, but still possible. According to his resumé, he had never been out of the United States. Each year was accounted for, in school, the army, teaching.

Unless, of course, the entire personality was fabricated. That was always possible. The spook could be on the university staff as a real person, or he could be using an entirely imaginary background. Anyone who could lay hands on fake American passports would have little trouble manufacturing whatever papers and records he might need. But I thought the spook was here as himself. When he'd planned to come to Lancaster he hadn't known that I would be on the scene, so why engage in an elaborate charade?

Daniel Riddell. Yes, I remembered meeting the Riddells at the University Playhouse. That had been a fun evening, a revival of a Noel Coward comedy. After it was over, Paul and I had walked home, hand in hand, unhurried, delighting in the autumn chill and the thin, high moon. Daniel Riddell was a big young man with untidy hair, a skimpy suit, and an awkward wife. His record was unspectacular though he had had one book published by a university press. According to the biographical data, he had married soon after completing high school. He and his wife had three children. Surely a man who would blow a plane out of the sky would not be so early domesticated. I hesitated, then placed the file atop the unlikely stack.

Stein, Milton. The picture showed a sensitive, almost melancholy face with a sleek moustache and somber eyes. Mr. Stein was thirty-four, a widower, a prolific critic with one book out on Salinger and another going to press in the spring. In 1966? He was an assistant professor in Chicago. So, Mr. Stein wasn't likely. I put his folder on top of Daniel Riddell's.

I was reaching for the last folder when the door to the hall opened.

"Do I have the wrong room, m'dear?"

I looked up and it was startling to see a face so recently and carefully studied. The original was older, saggier, more petulant than the photograph.

"You aren't the pretty young lady I talked to yesterday." He looked around. "But then, this isn't the right office, is it?"

"No, Mr. Dubois," I said quietly. "The office is next door."

He was inside and closing the door behind him and crossing to the table where I worked. I didn't like the look on his face, the aura he carried with him, of dim bars, sodden sleep, spurious laughter. He sat easily on the edge of the table and I could smell men's cologne and gin. This early in the morning? Or had it been a long night last night? An arduous night with the need of an early-morning pick-me-up?

"That's all right," he said smoothly. "You are even prettier." He watched me familiarly, as if he had known me for years. "You know my name," he said, flattered. "Which of my books have you read?"

"*Running Bright*," I lied.

"What did you think of it?"

"I thought it a very fine book."

"Death is always fascinating, isn't it?" he asked.

I stared at him, at his thick-lidded eyes and drooping mouth, and wondered if I looked at evil. Why had he come into this room? What did he want? Was he the one, and he couldn't resist harrying his victim?

"Death sometimes surprises his choice," I said steadily.

He leaned closer and the aroma of whiskey swirled around me.

"Little lady, that is a profound statement."

Nancy hurried in the door behind us. "Mrs. Hamilton, did I hear you call. . . . Oh, good morning, Mr. Dubois. You've met Mrs. Hamilton?"

He nodded formally. "Yes, I have now had that pleasure." His voice was silky and amused and his dark eyes watched me blandly. I was suddenly sure that he had known all the while who I was.

When they had both gone next door, ostensibly to search out some correspondence about a new textbook order for his course on the modern novel, I hesitated for a moment, then jumped up and locked both doors even though I knew it was an overreaction. What, after all, could happen in the middle of the morning in Felson Hall? But I felt safer with those doors locked. Mr. Dubois made my skin crawl.

I reread his biography. Yes, he could well be my pursuer. I would think more about him. Perhaps set a little trap.

But first I would finish the task I had set myself. There was one more folder to read.

Wyzanski, Roger J. His was a lean face with a close-cropped beard. He held his BA and MA degrees from California. He had studied at Cambridge, was a Vietnam veteran and the divorced father of two. There was no mention of Florence. His field was Milton and he had taught in Texas and Wisconsin. He was thirty-two. He was not too likely but he wasn't impossible, either. I added his folder to my stack of possibilities.

If I had the right instinct and luck, I had narrowed the pos-

129

sibilities to four. (*To four?* a mocking spirit inquired. In this city of forty-five thousand, you have narrowed it to four? How remarkable!) I wouldn't listen to that voice. I must be on the right track!

I pulled a sheet of scrap paper off a pile at the end of the table and wrote down the names. Ray Flood Dubois. Andrew Elwood Channing. Alan James. Roger Wyzanski.

I underscored Dubois's name, three thick black lines. And, best of all, abhorrent as I found him, I was not afraid of him! If he were the spook, I would be able to face him.

I quickly recorded the names, addresses, and telephone numbers of the four. I felt very close to success then. One of them was the spook, I felt sure of it. And, for an instant, I could empathize with his shock when he had come to Lancaster, for whatever purpose, and seen me. What bad luck he must have thought it that I should not only have survived the plane crash but that I should have come to hole here, in Lancaster.

It then occurred to me for the very first time to wonder why he had come to Lancaster, to the university.

Why on earth?

I laid down the sheet of paper and frowned. Once here, why, when he had seen me, didn't he leave? Make some excuse, illness, another job offer, something, and leave? Why should he stay and run the risk of my recognizing him?

For what possible reason had he been compelled to stay here — and to kill me to be safe?

I remembered the feeling that had enveloped me when I saw the notice in the Personals column and I made that hesitant, fearful search of my house. It was an overpowering sense of evil that had walked with me as I'd moved through a house suddenly inimical and alien.

Evil. A crawling, skin-prickling recognition of evil.

Why had that dimly remembered figure come to Lancaster?

I was so deep in thought, so intent upon probing this frightful question, that I didn't hear the knock at first.

Then it came again, louder, harder.

"Mrs. Hamilton, are you in there?"

I jumped up ran to the door, and opened it.

Nancy said, "I have a telephone message for you," and I knew from her face that she had thought the call a strange one.

I looked at her with still eyes. I looked with dreadful apprehension.

"A man called and said to tell you to please hurry straight home. He said Margaret needed you."

# XV

I must have said something to Nancy, must have made some kind of response. I know I grabbed up my purse and ran out of the office and down the stairs. I remember seeing Andrew's dark and handsome face but he turned away as I reached the second floor and didn't speak to me. I noticed that and thought how I had wronged him with my suspicions because, of course, he couldn't be here in Felson Hall and have Margaret. . . .

Margaret. My daughter, my baby, my lovely child. Why had I tried to meet danger on my own terms? Why hadn't I gone to the police and told them a killer was here, hunting me? What did it matter if I went to jail, if I lost Paul? What did anything matter beside Margaret's safety?

Oh Paul, Paul. I am so sorry. I thought Margaret was safe. I was sure Margaret was safe. Paul, I thought only I was in danger. Paul, forgive me.

Somehow I unlocked the Mercedes and drove home, tormented and brokenhearted. I flung myself out of the car and ran up the steps.

The front door was locked.

Somehow I hadn't expected it to be locked. I had thought. . . . Quickly I found the right key and unlocked the door. I reached back inside my purse for the Luger as I shoved the door in. I threw it back so hard that it slammed against the wall. The bang echoed in the foyer and then faded away to nothing, dying in the quiet of an empty house.

An empty house. It couldn't be empty. It mustn't be

empty. Where was Margaret?

I ran through the rooms, calling, my voice higher and higher, "Margaret! Margaret. Margaret, where are you?"

If she could hear me, she would answer. If she could hear. . . .

I ran up the stairs, pointing the Luger ahead of me. Her room was cold and still. The rumpled covers lay just as I had pulled them down to snatch her up and dress her last night. Her orange rabbit lay face down on the floor.

I checked every room. And I didn't find her. I turned to hurry back downstairs. I would call Nancy. Had she misunderstood the message? There could be no profit to anyone in luring me to an empty house.

Did I dare call the police? Could it have been a hoax, a ruse to get me here? My passionate longing that Margaret be safe was transformed into a conviction that she was! No, he couldn't have Margaret. He could not have followed Willamae with Margaret and at the same time have tried to force me off the road! This must be a trap!

I must hurry and shake free of it while there still was time. I was almost to the bottom of the stairs when he stepped out of the living room and looked up at me.

No hint of sound had warned me that he waited below. Had he been watching outside, waiting to make sure I came alone before he followed me through the opened door?

It was so shocking, so abrupt that it scarcely seemed real. I stopped and stared almost as if I thought that in the blink of time I would look and he would be gone.

But he was real.

I looked down at him and my heart wept. I had been wrong, wrong about Paul's department, wrong about Andrew, and, years before, I had been wrong about him.

Morgan watched me and his eyes were as bright and startlingly blue as I remembered them. But not truly as I remembered them. They had been merry, warm eyes in Florence, the eyes of a lover. The man who stood at the foot of my stairs looked with cold and watchful eyes.

I knew then. I knew.

What a credulous fool I had been! And, somehow, it was worse that I had clung to my memory of Morgan through the years, knowing I could never have him again, yet unable to truly put him behind me. It must have been a sham, right from the first. Had he laughed at my schoolgirlish adoration of him? Had he?

My hand held the Luger rock steady. It pointed at his heart, the heart that had never been mine. A fury such as I had never known swept me. My finger began to tighten against the trigger.

He saw his danger. The shock of it paled his smooth, still-unlined face. His voice was sharp and desperate and only just in time.

"Your little girl, Ann, don't you want to see her again? You fool, we have your little girl!"

Heart-stopping words.

My finger slipped off the trigger. The gun sagged to my side. Anguish and hopelessness welled with the same kind of horror that I'd learned of the destruction of the plane from Florence, the horror of loss, irreparable loss.

"Why?" I asked finally, my voice a thin thread of despair. "Why have you taken Margaret? Dear God, why?"

"Because you run too fast to catch, Ann. We knew you would come if we had your little girl."

"Have you hurt her?" The words were so hard to say.

"Of course not." The outrage in his voice was almost believable. Almost.

He was coming up the steps toward me.

I raised the Luger again and he stopped.

"If you've hurt Margaret, I will kill you, I swear, Morgan, if. . . ."

"Don't be absurd." He was impatient now. "There's no reason for Margaret to be hurt. If you do as I say, if you cooperate, there will be no danger for her. None at all. I promise you that."

Promises, promises.

"Oh, Morgan," I said bitterly, "I trusted you once, didn't I? You and your spook. And it was all a lie, wasn't it? You used me from the very first."

"No, Ann, no," he cried. "It wasn't that way at all." And his voice was warm now and his face open and frank. "It was an accident that the plane blew up. You must believe that."

Must I? Oh, Morgan, can you still think your charm so enduring? Have you such an overweening ego? But two can play that game.

"An accident?" I asked wonderingly, hopefully.

I saw the flicker in those brilliant blue eyes and worried that I had been too ingenuous, but no, his face relaxed and he moved confidently up to stand beside me. He took my elbow gently in one hand while he deftly disengaged the Luger from my limp fingers. He slipped the gun into his jacket pocket. "You won't need this," he said easily. "Now, let's go sit down and have a little talk."

He led me into my own living room and I hated the feel of his hand against my arm, but I managed a tremulous sideways smile.

I sat in the wingback chair as he lounged against the fireplace and spoke quickly and persuasively, his voice as young and golden as I remembered. But, oh, how carefully he watched me.

"First, let's be clear about your little girl, Ann. She's fine.

She's perfectly all right. And absolutely no harm will come to her — if you do as I say. Okay?'

"Where is she, Morgan?"

"Right where you thought she was. At your maid's mother's farm. And you needn't worry. Everything is going to turn out to your advantage."

His smile was as encouraging as when we'd sat across from the Santa Maria Novella and he so proudly told me how he had fixed it for me to make some exciting trips.

What had he fixed for me this time?

But I could school my face, too. I had had so much practice, five long years of it.

I asked hesitantly, hopefully, "How can it all work out, Morgan?"

The relief in his eyes at my malleability was fascinating to watch. I had been easy once. He was sure I would be easy again. Oh, Morgan, I owed you so much.

He was ebullient now, his fish so easily caught. "Nothing to it, Ann. Just a little help from you on the campus and your little girl will come home. Everything will be fine."

The fish has to fight the line for at least a little.

I shook my head. "I trusted you in Florence, Morgan. And you and your boss planned for me to be blown to bits."

"No, Ann, never! It wasn't that way at all!"

Wasn't it, Morgan? But I hid my bitter surety. I looked hopeful, eager to believe.

"You can't know how I grieved for you," he said huskily. (Oh, Morgan, you are laying it on a bit thick!) "That bomb wasn't meant to explode on the plane at all! It was to have been removed in Naples and substituted for a case checked through by one of the passengers." His mobile face was somber now. "I almost went crazy when I heard the plane had gone down."

136

"An accident," I repeated faintly.

"You'll never know how I suffered." Then quickly, eagerly, he said, "What a miracle it is that you are alive. I couldn't believe it when I saw you this fall. What happened that night in Florence?"

I told him how I had shoved the case beneath the seat and returned to the library and my shock the next day.

"Where did you go? What have you been doing since?"

His tone was perfect, full of delight in my escape, but his eyes were sharp and worried. Unspoken was the real question: Did you ever tell anyone, Ann, did you?

My lips were parting. I almost spoke, then sickness slid through me. Oh yes, I could say I had told Paul everything, convince Morgan, yes, I could do that.

And Paul would die.

My lips closed soundlessly, then brightly I began to talk, quickly sketching those years.

"So no one knows who you are," he said.

"No one but you," I responded.

His eyes slid away from mine.

I said tentatively, "But, Morgan, if I wasn't intended to die in that plane and if you're so glad I'm alive, then why have you been trying to kill me here in Lancaster?"

He frowned and for the first time I saw the faint, telltale lines of age. He was still handsome. I had to admit that, but the thick reddish hair curled more artfully now and there were flecks of gray in his beard. Had he noticed them yet? I doubted it. Odd how clearly I could see Morgan now. He ran a hand through his hair. It had been a charming gesture when he was twenty-three.

"It's been a damn mess," he said disarmingly.

That I could buy.

"You see, we're here in Lancaster. . . ."

And I heard the plural this time. That was how he had begun, too. "We have your little girl. . . ."

We.

"The spook?" I demanded, and I didn't try to keep the loathing out of my voice. "Is he in Lancaster too?"

Morgan nodded slowly.

"He wants to kill me," I said flatly.

Morgan threw up his hands. "God, Ann, I had no idea what he had in mind. I thought he was only trying to frighten you, with the letter and the ad and the snake. I didn't know he had tried to kill you until this morning! You see, he followed you from the airport while I followed your maid and your little girl. He promised me that if I caught them he would use them only to make sure you kept quiet about Florence. Then this morning, he told me you had to be killed."

He saw my expression and hurried on, "But it's all right now, Ann. I've convinced him that you will cooperate and that you can be a terrific help."

The spook had wanted me dead. I knew that. But why? I studied Morgan thoughtfully. "You've both been here since September?"

He nodded.

"Then why did he suddenly decide I had to . . . die?"

"I'm not sure," Morgan replied, "but I think it's because you came to the art museum. Do you remember? A week ago Sunday."

I remembered. I remembered very clearly.

"Until you came there, I had convinced him that there was no danger of you seeing me because our paths wouldn't cross."

"You're on the art faculty then."

"Yes, and when you came to that showing, I just missed walking into you. That must have worried him. He has been keeping you under a close watch."

"Who is he, Morgan?"

Morgan looked uncomfortable. "I'd better not say, Ann. You know him. You didn't recognize him when you met him this fall. He didn't recognize you either from that night in Florence."

So Morgan's partner didn't remember me from that long-ago night in Florence. And I hadn't recognized him either. But we had met.

"Where did I meet him, Morgan?"

Morgan looked evasive. "One place and another. Parties. The President's Reception."

The President's Reception. Last Friday evening in the Union Ballroom. A formal dinner and dance to welcome new faculty members and their wives or husbands. It was one of the major social events of the fall even though times and mores were changing and many younger faculty members were disdainful of the pomp and circumstance. Disdainful, perhaps, but they came, the young wives in brocaded pants suits, their bearded and curled husbands in velvet jackets and bright trousers. It was a huge, unwieldy conglomeration, drawing together all of the disciplines for the only time in the year, petroleum engineering and modern-dance faculty meeting over the punch bowl. Everyone was there. In an old-fashioned way, it was always a very enjoyable evening. This year President Morris had insisted upon retaining the receiving line but had agreed to the novelty of a rock band at one end of the great ballroom. Once my official duties were through, I had joined Paul and we had moved slowly and happily from group to group, greeting old friends, welcoming newcomers.

"At the President's Reception," I repeated. "Then he is a faculty member, too. And he is in Paul's department."

139

Morgan nodded uneasily.

So I had met my enemy that night. It had been such a happy evening. So many old friends to greet, Arthur and Mary Lou McAllister, back from a sabbatical in England; John Abelard, tanned from a summer spent digging in New Mexico; dear Julian, who overwhelmed everyone with his height, his irreverent and often scandalous conversation and his enduring charm. To be truthful, I had not been as interested in meeting new people, duty once served, as in greeting old friends. Now I tried desperately to picture the milling throng, to recall those to whom I had spoken.

How many of Paul's new people had come through the receiving line? Andrew, of course, and Alan James and Dubois. I didn't remember Roger Wyzanski. So three of my four had spoken with me. Three. But it might as well be three hundred. What difference did it make who he was, what he called himself, why he had come to Lancaster? My luck was out. He had my little girl and there was nothing in this world I could do about it.

"Look, Ann, there's no point in worrying about who he is or where he is. It's better if you never know. It's the only way I can work it out, Ann, for you and for Margaret. But, if you help, he's promised that he will let Margaret go and leave you alone. Please, Ann, trust me."

Said the spider to the fly.

No, I'd never be fool enough to trust Morgan again. But let him think I trusted him. Then, perhaps, somehow, some way, I could break free from him and get help for Margaret and Willamae.

"You want my help," I said slowly. "Why? What is there I could do for you in Lancaster?"

He swept his hand through his hair again. "It's a political job, Ann. You don't need to know the whys and wherefores.

Your part will be very easy."

"Political," I repeated. "But it has nothing to do with the CIA?"

He smiled a little at that.

"And it didn't in Florence, either."

"Right."

"That was just to impress a schoolgirl, wasn't it?"

He shrugged. "Don't worry about it, Ann. If you'll just come along and follow my directions, everything will be fine."

I could feel the tension in him. He was getting impatient.

"Come on now, Ann, we don't have much time."

"But how can I be sure that Margaret is really all right?" I demanded sharply.

"You can't be sure," he snapped. "But you don't have any choice. And, as soon as you do your job, I'll take you to her."

"No, Morgan."

He stared at me in surprise.

"No, Morgan." And my voice was harsh. "No, not later. Now."

# XVI

He was sullen. He drove the Mercedes jerkily and too fast. I knew from his tight-drawn mouth that he was afraid. Not of me, of course. He had feared me that instant when I'd aimed the Luger at his heart, but that was past and in his mind I was no threat. No, he was afraid of his companion in terror who had told him quite specifically how to capture me and what to make me do.

And the players weren't keeping to the script.

Morgan swore at me. He threatened, warning that he couldn't answer for Margaret's safety if I persisted in my idiocy. But I was obdurate. I would go no place, do nothing, until I had seen Margaret. I had to see Margaret, hold her, know she was . . . alive.

I had asked him, "Did you leave Margaret with . . . him?"

"No, no," he said quickly.

"Then how could you leave her and Willamae?" I demanded sharply.

"I tied them up."

I closed my eyes for a moment. Margaret tied. She would be so frightened.

"I had to," Morgan said defensively. "He was going to check on them while I was gone."

"If he was coming to the farmhouse," I said bleakly, "then I must see her."

He had to give in. That or kill me, so we drove through the cold gray morning, Morgan hunched angrily over the wheel.

As we drove I occasionally glanced down at the small suit-case at my feet. Its contents puzzled me but seemed some-what reassuring. Morgan had shepherded me up the stairs and to the master bedroom.

At my closet, he pointed at the rack of dresses. "Where's the one you wore to the President's Reception?"

"At the cleaners."

He directed me to pick out another dress that would be suitable for a luncheon. That seemed simple enough and cer-tainly not sinister. I chose a soft raspberry wool with a boat neck. He waited impatiently while I gathered up the accesso-ries. Once packed, he hurried me downstairs and out to the Mercedes.

He drove fast right from the first. Once on the expressway, the Mercedes hurtled along on the rain-slick pavement.

I studied his profile. Even in the dismal gray morning, his red hair gleamed and the line of his forehead and cheek was handsome. True, there might be a hint of weakness in the drooping line of his mouth, but nothing to suggest his corrupt soul. He was sleek, his sweater a poem in cashmere, his double knit sports coat and slacks beautifully tailored. He lived, and in the Bay of Naples bone and flesh from the shat-tered plane had long since disintegrated.

The Mercedes held its speed until he slowed to swing down the exit ramp and onto Highway 87, a two-lane road. Then he accelerated again.

We rode in silence for five minutes, ten. I rubbed my hand tiredly against my face, then asked the question that I had carried for so many years. "Morgan, why did he have me carry a bomb aboard that plane?"

"The case was to have been substituted for one carried by a passenger, a Fascist who was getting too much power to suit one of our clients."

One of our clients. So he and the "spook" had been part-ners all along. I didn't even bother to question his fiction that the bomb had been intended to explode at a later time.

I stared at his handsome profile. He had answered so easily. What did it matter to him that a crying baby and a handsome, gray-haired businessman died too? And so many others.

Morgan was watching the speedometer now. Not far ahead, I saw the highway sign, SH 14, and knew we were on our way to Willamae's mother's farm. That made me feel better. They must be there, they must be safe, else why should Morgan bother to take me?

For the first time since I'd learned that Margaret was a prisoner, I took some hope. If Margaret and Willamae were truly alive, if they still were safe, perhaps there really was a chance that they might be set free if I cooperated. Or, perhaps at some point I might be able to get help for them. I no longer worried about protecting my identity. It didn't matter. Noth-ing mattered but saving Margaret and Willamae.

Morgan turned onto the state highway and it was a narrow blacktop, slick as glass from the rains, but the Mercedes clung to that insolent surface without hesitation.

I was watching now for the little country store that would mark our next turn. The blacktop was a winding, swooping road. The store sat on a rise. It boasted a single gasoline pump, a patch of gravel for a drive, and a Rainbow bread sign over the weathered gray door. The screens were tattered and several window panes patched. We slowed and turned heavily into the narrow, graveled road which twisted and turned from the outset.

The twisting and turning reminded me of the care I had taken en route to the airport the night before. I had been so sure I was not followed and yet I must have been, for Morgan trailed Willamae and Margaret to the farm and his partner had tried to force me off the road to Lancaster.

"Morgan, how did you and your partner follow Margaret and me to the airport?"

"We didn't, Ann. We met you there."

"But how could you have possibly known where I was going?"

He smiled. "Not black magic, though it must seem near enough sometimes. My partner really was in the CIA once, till he decided the pay was too low and the fringe benefits lousy. He put a bug on your phone a couple of weeks ago. He's a careful man."

My telephone bugged. So my call to Willamae had boomeranged. I had been outmaneuvered at every turn.

Then we were at the half track which angled off to the left. It was almost hidden by overhanging branches.

The Mercedes filled the narrow way. Bushes scraped against her sides. Branches met overhead. It was as dim and gray and funereal as the interior of a long-deserted stone church. It was the longest half mile I ever endured.

The track ended abruptly and the Mercedes plunged out of the branched tunnel into a featureless yard, frightening a half dozen chickens into awkward flight. Morgan braked and the Mercedes slipped sideways on the grassless, clayey surface.

I knew as I looked, even in that first fleeting glimpse when the eye records but does not evaluate, that it was wrong, all wrong. I was opening the door and tumbling out and I was terribly, terribly frightened.

It was an incredibly narrow house, two storys but as thin as an obliquely seen house done by Wyeth. The house almost merged into the misty grayness of the morning, its weathered, slanting wood the color of slate. The second-story windows were boarded over. The ground-floor windows were patched with cardboard and tape.

No light shone. There was no sound but the rustle and cluck of the chickens. And, most frightening of all, there was only one car parked in that desolate yard, Willamae's shabby VW.

I was running toward that unmoving front door. Behind me I heard Morgan, and his call was as loud as a shout in the deathly quiet.

"Wait! Wait, Ann. Wait!"

I was almost to the rickety steps when I stumbled to a stop and stared in horror at the lifeless mound just at the corner of the house. I stared and moaned deep in my throat.

The shot had blown away part of the German shepherd's muzzle. The collie's chest was matted with blood. They lay in an unmoving heap.

"Margaret," I whispered.

Somehow I managed the last few steps to the porch and moved up the rickety stairs. Morgan had stopped behind me and I knew he too was staring at the dogs.

The house was deathly quiet.

Nothing moved in the dimness of that crowded living room. No one called out, either in fear or welcome. Nothing, nothing. It was such a small space to be so filled, three chairs, a sofa covered by a worn afghan, a wooden table, a sewing machine and, in one corner, a dressmaker's mannequin. An old iron stove filled another corner. Next to it was a tin sink. On the floor was an aluminum bucket, mute testimony to a well.

"Margaret!" It was a cry of despair.

"He must have taken them . . ." Morgan began, and even I could hear the honest bewilderment in his voice. So Morgan had thought they would be here.

Then I saw the ladder that climbed up to a square opening in the ceiling. I ran to it.

How many rungs were there? Eight, perhaps nine. I climbed up and hauled myself through the opening and then I saw them.

I never remembered crossing that little space and leaning over the bed and trying to gather up that still little figure, her soft brown hair limp against the patched white pillowcase.

"Margaret, oh Margaret, Margaret."

Nor did I ever remember how long it took me to realize that a strand of clothesline held her tight against the lumpy mattress and to understand that she was warm and lightly, almost imperceptibly, breathing.

Dear God, she was alive.

I thought it true, then feared again and frantically held that feather-light wrist and hunted for a pulse, but could find nothing. I put my face close to hers, so pale and shadowed, and felt so very faintly the soft caress of her breath.

I brushed the silky hair back from her face and gently touched the pale cheeks. They were warm and now I could hear the slow but even breaths. It was not, of course, a natural sleep. I ran my hands down her arms and found the mark of the hypodermic needle in her left arm.

Willamae lay in the center of the bed and she too slept the deep, unnatural sleep of the drugged. But she had also been hurt. Her right cheek was puffy and blood streaked. I quickly reached out to touch her wrist. The pulse was slow but strong and rhythmic.

The clothesline crossed Margaret and Willamae and a heavy, older woman whom I knew must be Willamae's mother.

It was the clothesline which reassured me. It not only

encircled them at chest and thigh, but each was also bound hand and foot.

Why tie them so securely if they were left to die?

But what if he had given them too much of the drug? Margaret was so small. She only weighed thirty-seven pounds. Had he bothered to think of that? Had he calculated the dose to her size?

I bent my face toward her and once again felt the wispy breath against my cheek. It was even breathing although slow, so slow. She was all right. Wasn't she?

"Okay now," Morgan said nervously. "You've seen them. They're here. They're okay. And it looks to me like they've been lucky."

I looked up at him. "What do you mean?"

He ran a hand through his thick red hair. "I left them here this morning all comfortably tied up downstairs. So, if they'd played it cool, they'd still be down there and not drugged. It's clear to me what happened. She," and he nodded toward Willamae, "must have worked loose. I suppose she had just made it outside when my partner came. He told me he would check on them while I waited for you at your house. He came, she let the dogs loose. I don't suppose she realized he had a gun. He had to shoot the dogs, of course." He shook his head. "She's lucky he didn't shoot her too."

I thought Morgan was right on that. Anyone who would blow up a plane full of innocent people to kill a political enemy wouldn't hesitate to gun down a woman who threatened him. Bless Willamae, bless her for trying.

"So they're up here and they're okay. Let's get out of here."

"How can I be sure they're all right, be sure he didn't give Margaret too much of the drug?"

"How can. . . . For God's sake, Ann, what can you expect?

148

Look, I brought you out here. You've seen them. They're still alive. Now, if you want them to stay that way, it's up to you. And we've got to hurry."

I could hear the strain in his voice, but still I lingered beside her bed. How could I leave her, her breaths so faint as to be almost imperceptible?

"Ann, listen to me," and his voice was urgent, compelling. "We have to go. Now. Time's running out. Margaret will be all right. Don't you see, he could have killed her already — but he didn't. Why should he kill Margaret?"

Perhaps, I thought, for the same reason that he had planned my death that long-ago night in Florence. A dead witness was no witness at all. I knew I had been meant to die on that airplane. It had been no "premature" explosion. I could remember so well those definite instructions about the passport. That dark figure, so briefly seen at the foot of the library steps, had never intended for me to return to Florence. He didn't care how many he killed to achieve his goal, whatever dark and evil design it might be.

A plane had lifted away from a wet runway and people had laughed and read magazines and settled back for short naps. A baby had cried. The plane flew truly through the star-spangled night and people made plans and thought about a future which never came.

No, I had no illusions about Morgan or his spook. They would deal with me and mine as best suited them. They might keep an agreement. They might not. All I could know with surety was that Margaret and Willamae and her mother still lived at this point in time. I could be sure of nothing else, but, from my position of weakness, I couldn't demand more. All I could do was go with Morgan and somehow at some moment try to get help. I knew how slim my chance was.

But it was the only chance I had.

149

# XVII

The full-throttle skidding drive away from the farm was a horror. Ink-black clouds diminished the horizon. Brilliant flashes of lightning splintered the darkening sky. Thunder exploded. The rain began.

The Mercedes careened around curves, a magnificent machine in desperate hands. Morgan's face in the full gray light of the storm was pale and haggard; all youthfulness had fled. He drove as if he were possessed by demons, spurred by unspeakable consequences should he be late.

The intensity of this fear was so striking that for the first time in the long morning I did not think about Margaret and Willamae. For the first time, I made myself think about what was going to happen next.

Where were we going? And why? And what did Morgan and his spook want me to do?

"Morgan, why must we go so fast?" I asked sharply after a frightful moment when the Mercedes swung almost out of control.

He didn't look at me. He hunched a little closer to the wheel. "Ann, you don't know him. If we don't get back to town in time. . . ."

I watched him, seeing him without the golden aura he had worn in Florence and in all my dreams of long years since. I saw a man of thirty-odd years hunched over a steering wheel, a nerve flickering in his cheek, his hands white-knuckled on the dark plastic wheel. A dangerous man.

Back to town in time for . . . what?

I didn't know where we were going. I didn't know what they wanted me to do. But I knew, in my heart, that it would be evil.

I must stop him. But if I did, I would lose Margaret.

We weren't far from town when I wondered what would be my odds of surviving a crash. The Mercedes had the road to herself in the swirling rain.

I looked at the speedometer. The needle hovered right at seventy! The curling black ribbon of the road was as greasy as an oiled iron skillet. He could not stop suddenly, not possibly. If I yanked the wheel there would be no way he could control the Mercedes.

But I could not help Margaret and Willamae from the tangle of a wrecked car, even if I were in any condition to help them. Besides, to destroy Morgan was to meet only half the threat, and it might indeed be the lesser half. What good would it do to stop Morgan — and leave a ravening tiger free? No, this was not the time to try.

Oh, Janey, you dreaming, wishful fool, I told myself bitterly. What makes you think there will be a right moment?

I moved uncomfortably in the seat and watched his strained profile. Where were we going at such a breakneck pace? Even wondering about our destination was begging the question, was part of the mind's defensive response to intolerable pressure.

It didn't matter where we were going. What mattered was why.

All right, Janey, lay it out. Morgan and his friend intended to use their possession of Margaret and Willamae to force me to do . . . something ugly, something evil.

Surely there was a limit to what they could expect a hostage to do, could force a hostage to do. Whatever it was, I made one vow. I would not hurt innocent people, not ever again, not for Margaret nor Willamae nor myself.

I would not carry a valise aboard an airplane.

We were in Lancaster now and Morgan was forced to slow as the rain became a cascade. It was raining so hard when we reached the Sinclair Street parking lot on the campus that the gutters were awash. It was impossible to see more than a few feet ahead.

The parking lot was full. I could have told Morgan that it would be. Even on a fine day the likelihood of finding a parking space was slim. It didn't exist when it rained. But he didn't swing out the front drive when we made full circle. Instead, he turned into the first row of parking and, at its end, drove the Mercedes up and over the curb and slammed to a stop beside a weeping willow tree.

"Morgan, you can't park here!"

"Shut up! Get your case and hurry."

I was drenched the moment I stepped out of the car. He locked it, then hurried around the car to get me. We ran, heads down, through the icy sheets of rain. His fingers dug viciously into my elbow. It was raining so hard we literally could not see our way, and the water ran as high as our ankles in the paved patio behind the Union. We ran hard along the back of the Union, then swerved to our left, and I knew Morgan was heading for the steps leading up to a little-used side entrance.

At the top of the steps we cannoned full force into a tall, caped figure and I realized with a spurt of joy that it was Julian St. John. We would all have gone sprawling but for Julian's cat-quick response. He grabbed the railing with his right hand to catch himself and with his left hooked my arm, saving me from a backward topple. Morgan, of course, still gripped my other arm. For an instant we made an awkward tableau, and then we shifted and stepped apart.

Morgan's hold on my arm tightened warningly. I knew as clearly as if he had spoken that he was reminding me that Margaret's life hung in the balance. If I tried to ask for help, if somehow Julian and I together could overpower Morgan I would lose Margaret. And what chance would Julian and I have anyway against the Luger in Morgan's pocket?

I tried to smile up at Julian. Dear Julian. At six foot six, he towered above everyone. With his drooping moustache and slightly hunched stance, he always attracted notice. Paul had told me that during World War II Julian, an Englishman, parachuted into Greece and led a band of partisans hated and feared above all others by the Germans. He was, my husband said, an incredibly brave man. He was also a man who did as he wished and never worried that he might look foolish or absurd and, somehow, no matter what extravagant gesture he made, no one ever ridiculed him. There was a thrust to his jaw and a quality in his eyes that commanded deference.

"My dear Janey," Julian boomed, patting my wet shoulder, "what are you doing out in this deluge? Surely only duty would drive one forth today. Ah yes, I imagine you are on your way to the reception for the defense minister. I am going there myself. Here, let's get out of the rain."

He pulled out the door and Morgan and I wedged through and then we were all standing, dripping, making irregular puddles on the marble foyer. A narrow hall stretched to the right and left. It was empty. Stairs climbed to our right.

Julian slipped off his waterproof cape and was taking off his cap while he looked at Morgan and me with sharp, curious eyes.

"How did you happen to be caught out without your raincoat, Janey?"

Morgan watched him with still, cold blue eyes. His hand

slipped into his jacket pocket.

"Too many things to think about today," I chattered. As I talked I tried to move Morgan down the hall. "I'm on the committee to greet the defense minister." I hadn't at that moment an idea in the world who the defense minister was. I didn't care. I only knew I must move us down the hall, talking, dissembling, or Morgan might shoot Julian. "In fact, we must hurry. This gentleman has been kind enough to help on the arrangements. He represents the public information office." I looked down at my watch, then said briskly, "My goodness, I had no idea it was this late. We must hurry." I thrust my free hand into Julian's and said heartily, "It's been so good to see you, George," and I pressed my index finger hard against his wrist, feeling an incongruous mixture of terror at making an effort to signal and embarrassment at resorting to such an infantile and probably useless attempt. Then, quickly, quickly, I dropped Julian's hand and pushed past him to start up the stairway. Morgan hesitated, then let himself be pulled along with me. We left Julian standing in the small foyer, looking after us. His face, as they used to say in the Sunday supplements, was a study.

Morgan looked back and saw him watching, and I felt Morgan slow and start to turn. I walked a little faster. Morgan looked at me, looked back down the stairs at Julian, then hurried to catch up.

"Who was that?" he asked tensely.

"George Julian St. Clair. A drama professor."

Morgan relaxed at that. "Yeah. That's what he looks like." His head swiveled toward me. "You look like hell. What can you do about your hair?"

I shrugged. "Not much."

"Can't you brush it or something? You can't look like a drowned rat."

154

And why not? I started to ask. But I didn't bother. I was shivering uncontrollably, in part because I was chilled through and in part because it had been such a close thing with Julian.

Morgan had my elbow again and was pushing me along ahead of him. He looked at his watch and began to move a little faster.

"For heaven's sake, Morgan, slow down. What's all the rush?"

'We only have fifteen minutes before the defense minister is supposed to arrive."

"What does that have to do with us?"

His bright blue eyes slid over my face. "This is where you play your part, Ann. This is the price for your little girl."

I stopped in the hallway, stared at his old-young face, looked into his shuttered eyes, and knew I had come to the end of the line. I was not going to be able to save Margaret or Willamae or myself. The price was going to be too high.

"Goddamnit, Ann, hurry!"

"Why? What is it that you want me to do?"

"Look, it's simple. All you have to do is be an official greeter and hand the minister a present."

"A present?"

"Right. A present. A nice present in a white box wrapped up in blue paper with a silver bow. Honest to God, that's all there is to it."

"If it's so simple, so easy, if the box doesn't hold a bomb. . . ."

"Bomb!" he interrupted. He shook his head vigorously. "Ann, it's nothing like that."

"Isn't it?" I asked skeptically. "Then why all this frenzied effort on your part? Would you go to all the trouble to kidnap Margaret and Willamae if all you want me to do is hand a man an innocent box?"

His eyes met mine for an instant, then slid away. He tugged at his beard. "It's not an innocent box," he said softly. "It's going to land you in a jam, Ann, but you can talk your way out of it."

"What is in the box, Morgan? What?"

"A head."

I stared at him, looking deep into those sea-blue eyes. "Dear God, why?"

"To cause a scandal."

"I don't understand, Morgan."

"It's very simple, Ann. It's going to place the minister in a very tight spot. The head belonged to a quite young, quite pretty secretary at the Lebanese Embassy. The defense minister has just spent a month in Washington, conferring at the Pentagon and making speeches to Zionist groups."

"Zionist groups," I repeated.

"Right, dear. The defense minister is from Israel and his appearance on the campus today is sponsored by Hillel Foundation. And it's going to be nothing but an uproar when he is presented with the head of a nice young Arab girl, who, by the way, was engaged to a boy back home in Beirut. The newspapers will go wild and the gossip and speculation will ruin him — and probably bring down the present government in Israel."

"How ugly."

He shrugged. "Do you like it better than a bomb?"

"Yes," I said tiredly. Ugly as it was, it was better than a bomb. And knowing this, I saw that everything, their kidnapping of Margaret and Willamae, their capture of me, had a hideous logic. I saw too that perhaps they really meant it when they said they would let us go. Once I had finished my task.

"So come on, Ann. Let's get it done." He took my hand and began to pull me along with him.

We were on the second floor of the Union building. This wing held offices and smaller meeting rooms. The major reception areas and the grand ballroom were on the third floor. He paused just before we reached the wide, main staircase.

"Here we are." He opened the door to Room 25 and hustled me inside.

I looked around curiously and couldn't imagine why we were here. Then I saw Morgan take a key from his pocket and lock the door.

When he turned toward me, I asked him, "What am I supposed to tell the police when all hell breaks loose?"

"You're going to tell them that you received a telephone call from a man who said he was calling from the president's office and wanted you to present a memento to Defense Minister Levin in your capacity as an official greeter," Morgan said glibly. "You were told to pick up the wrapped present in Room 25 and give it to Defense Minister Levin at the end of the official reception, just before he was scheduled to make the luncheon address."

"What if they don't believe me?"

He shrugged. "What does it matter what they believe? They can't prove otherwise and you have no connection with any political group that could conceivably have engineered it. Why shouldn't they believe you?"

Yes indeed, why shouldn't they believe the wife of a respected department chairman? Why shouldn't they accept it? And Morgan and his friend would be free to spread their evil here or elsewhere.

"But when it's over, Ann, you'll get Margaret back."

Yes, then they would be safe.

Once they were safe, however, what could prevent me from telling the police the truth?

It was as if he read my mind. "I can understand that you might be tempted then to go to the police. But don't try it, Ann. He told me to make it clear that he would kill Margaret if you go to the police. Sooner or later."

I turned away from Morgan and gripped the back of a straight chair. I would never be free of him or his spook. From now until the day I died, I would be bound to them, forever linked by the fiery deaths of fifty-four people.

"So just do your part and keep quiet, Ann, and everything will be fine. Now, get dressed. Time is running out."

I put the suitcase on top of one of the chair seats and opened it to lift out the raspberry dress. Such a beautiful dress. I remembered the bright day in September when I'd bought it and how I'd admired it, turning this way and that in the dressing room, liking its soft color and the way it curved against my body, thinking that Paul would be pleased.

I would never be able to wear it again.

Hurrying now, my fingers awkward against the wet buttons of my blouse, I loosened it down the front. I hesitated, then stolidly slipped it off. I shut away the memory of those long-ago days when I had undressed so eagerly for Morgan. I yanked up the raspberry dress and pulled it over my head. Then I stepped out of my slacks. My bra and panties still clung damply to me but with the magic of nylon they were beginning to dry. It took only a moment more to pull up the pantyhose and step into the heels. I almost didn't bother to pick up and slip into the loops the heavy braided belt with the soft furry tassels. But I did because habit is hard to overcome. A dress is not worn without its belt. So I quickly threaded the thick cordlike belt and looped and tied it. Then I turned to pick up my purse but stopped, and my hands fell to my sides and I didn't think of it again.

I had dressed quickly. Morgan was not watching me. In fact, he didn't even notice me turn around. He was absorbed in his task, lifting a gift box out of a large gray toolbox. He lifted it so slowly and gently and carefully.

He knelt, in profile to me, by the toolbox, which he must have drawn out from beneath a chair. A sturdy padlock dangled in the toolbox's hasp. Morgan had the gift box out now and was setting it down on the waxed parquet floor. Then he reached into the toolbox again to lift out something small and black. I thought that perhaps it was a transistor radio but just as I saw it Morgan sensed my watching eyes and looked up. He slipped the black object into his coat pocket.

"So you're ready. Do something to your hair and let's get this over with."

He closed the toolbox and shoved both it and my small case, in which I had dumped my discarded clothes, beneath a chair.

He picked up the gift box, beautifully wrapped in soft blue-gray paper and topped with a silvery bow, and stood and watched me as I tried to redo my wet and draggled hair. Finally I scooped it back in a bun and jabbed bobby pins into it until it held.

Morgan was waiting for me at the door, the gift box in his hands.

# XVIII

The box was heavy in my hands. I tried very hard not to appraise that weight, not to picture the contents. I carried it a little out in front of me and walked as rapidly as I could up the broad central steps, part of an eager crowd hurrying toward the third floor and the ballroom.

I felt abnormally alive to people, to the assorted beings at this moment so close to me. It was not a homogeneous gathering. Affluent matrons, hatted and befurred, were matched in equal number by heavily bearded, denim-clad students. Rumpled professors, tidy administrators and trim members of the League of Women Voters flowed up the stairs.

It was a remarkable turnout for a weekday noon luncheon and nothing short of fantastic considering the weather. But now that I knew the speaker's identity I wasn't surprised. The new Israeli defense minister was blessed in equal parts with charisma, a superb sense of timing, and a talent for the spectacular. He had charmed Washington with his handsome hawk-like profile, ingratiated himself with several very powerful senators, and dominated news-service copy so much that a disgruntled pro-Arab columnist accused his fellow reporters of tampering with the world balance of power.

The crowd moved fairly smoothly. At the landing I risked a quick backward glance and far below me I saw the bright sheen of Morgan's hair. Then I started up the final flight of stairs, remembering Morgan's hurried last words, "I'll be behind you, love. But don't think you can pull a clever trick and get away — because I won't be the only one watching you. He'll be here too. And believe me, Ann, if you don't present the box just as you've been told, well, he has it planned. He'll get back to the farmhouse before you — and Ann, you won't want to see Margaret then."

Ugly words. Unimaginable horrors only too easily imagined. Please, God, not to Margaret, please, please. And the bitter knowledge that innocence is no defense, provides no security, and the painful, doubly painful now, memory of the five little boys in their gray suits that long-ago night in Florence.

"Janey, oh, Janey! How fun to see you. Where are you sitting?"

I stretched my mouth into a smile and wondered that no one saw the haunting behind my face.

"Hello, Karen," I managed. "I wish I could join you, but I've a job to do first," and I raised the package up.

She nodded. "We'll be at the far table on the left. Come along if you can."

Come along, I thought grimly, and bring your head with you. But my mind recoiled at picturing that moment when the defense minister opened the package. I should be thinking, readying a response. What would be the appropriate demeanor? Dear God, what was I going to do?

I was at the double doors leading into the ballroom when a hand reached out and touched my arm.

"Excuse me, ma'am, may I have your ticket, please?"

I looked blankly at the handsome, olive-skinned boy who had stopped me.

"Everyone is supposed to have a ticket," he said finally, and a dull flush climbed his cheeks.

My heart thudded. It was another long moment before I

thought to point to the name tag, survivor of the President's Reception. "I'm not attending the luncheon," I said pleasantly. "I'm here to present this . . ." I paused, then continued as steadily and evenly as possible, "memento to the defense minister on behalf of the university. Did the committee not inform you?"

The young man turned an even deeper red. "No, ma'am. I'm sorry. I wouldn't have stopped you if I'd known. Please, go right on in."

"Thank you," I said. "Thank you very much." But I wondered as I stepped inside the huge room. Had Morgan made a mistake, forgotten to give me a ticket? Or had it been deliberate, to impress the ticket taker with the identity of the box carrier? I felt like a puppet yanked a step at a time across a stage.

Morgan was coming in the doors now. And he had a ticket.

I looked across the huge room. Beyond the seemingly endless ranks of white-draped tables I saw the raised dais. Near it was a thick knot of people, a circular mass bunched around one man.

Morgan was standing not more than five feet from me. His face was impassive, his eyes slid past me without a hint of recognition, but his head inclined in an almost infinitesimal motion toward the speaker's table and the clot of people.

I took a deep breath and began to walk. I was moving past Morgan, almost even with him, when a lanky, long-haired boy, his camera dangling from his hand, shoved past me, jostling me. I stumbled forward, my arms outthrust. For an instant the gift box teetered on the ends of my fingers. Somehow I managed to catch it up, to grab it before it fell, but in the instant before I once again had it secure in my arms, I saw Morgan jump back and fling his hands up before his face.

My back was to him by the time I recovered my balance.

Somehow I managed to keep on walking though my legs were trembling. The people around me, some hurrying toward the speaker's stand, others taking seats at the long tables, kept on talking. No one had noticed Morgan's instinctive reaction.

No one but me.

I knew now. I was a fool. A fool again. How could I ever have believed him, believed anything he said! And I had. Deep down, I had held to the hope that it would all come right, that Margaret and Willamae would be safe if I did as I was told. But it was all a lie. A lie here. A lie in Florence. He had known about the bomb then. He knew now. Morgan had known I walked toward death twice now — and he hadn't cared. Yes, I would know Morgan in heaven or in hell, always. I would remember him as few first loves are remembered.

One foot before the other, I walked ahead. How could I ever have believed in Morgan? And now it was too late. I was the instrument of death. For how many this time? God alone knew. Myself, of course, and the handsome, dynamic man from Israel. How often he must have been near death before. In the Six Day War. In the campaigns against the terrorists. How far he had come to meet death! Halfway around the world. How strange to meet death in this antiseptic, pastel-hued banquet room!

I was still on the far side of the huge room, a long way from the defense minister. How long could I reasonably take to cross that space?

I slowed and deliberately moved a little to my right, where the crowd was thickest. And I began to look for a way out. It is incredible how the mind refuses to accept finality, incredible how it will continue to search and think and try to find escape even as the distance shortens and it comes closer and closer to the final moment.

The wall to my right, the south end of the room, was two stories high and void of doors. An occasional huge perpendicular window broke the monotony of the wall.

Could I break a pane? Throw the bomb out the window?

Out and down upon some unsuspecting pedestrians? But it was raining, God love us, raining sheets and torrents. Perhaps no one would be crossing. Perhaps.

I had walked another ten feet now. I was only half the room away from the minister.

I wanted so badly to run and smash glass and fling away the package. Wouldn't that be better than having it explode in the midst of the people crowding around the defense minister?

But I could not destroy innocent people to save myself or Margaret. And if I hurried, ran and hurried, why couldn't I reach the farmhouse before him? Morgan had the keys to the Mercedes but there was another set in a metallic holder beneath the left front fender. I would take the package with me.

I looked at the far end of the room. This wasn't impossible at all! I would walk toward the defense minister. Yes, I would walk so close I could see his bony face and dark burning eyes and he would never know how near his fate had stepped. At the last possible moment, I would dash for the fire exit, push through the heavy door, and run down the steps, driven by a far greater care and despair than would ever move Morgan or his friend. I would reach the car before them and I would race that powerful black car as she had never been raced before.

I had it all worked out and then I turned a little to my left to look back at Morgan. He was still standing by the door, watching me, his face taut and worried. Again, this time forcefully, he inclined his head toward that eddying crowd of people.

His hand, his right hand, was in his jacket pocket.

That was the pocket in which he had dropped that black plastic case, the one so similar in size to a transistor radio.

I turned slowly back toward the speaker's stand, slowly because I could move no other way against the hurtful pressure in my chest. I tried to draw in breath, pull it past the paralysis of terror.

Poor Janey. Poor, stupid, unclever Janey. They've ringed you round, my dear. They didn't take a chance that the rabbit might run. The dogs always get the rabbit, one way or another. How could I have imagined that they would leave it to chance, gamble on whether Janey Hamilton would cross that floor and unsuspectingly thrust a package upon that lean and handsome man in the midst of his admiring throng. Oh no, they always bet on a sure thing.

Hand the nice man the package, Janey, and as his brown hand stretches forth politely to accept it, Morgan's finger presses the switch and unseen, blackly magical, the electrical impulses spin through the air, and, abruptly, the bomb detonates. A flash of smoke. A dart of flame. A crashing, thunderous explosion and the handsome Israeli and the slender fair woman are gone. Blown out of existence as completely as though they'd never been.

I walked slowly forward. If I went too close to the defense minister Morgan would detonate the bomb. But if I ran away, if he realized that I knew what the package contained, he would detonate it anyway. He could not let me reach the police. Not now. Not ever.

My hands were wet and slippery against the slick blue paper. Sweat trickled down my back and sides.

A few feet away, I saw an old friend, Callie Bristow. Tall, big-boned Callie painted vigorous, haunting still lifes, windmills abandoned years earlier, an office at dawn, a child's toy

165

in a sandpile. She managed her huge family, a husband and seven children, with great good cheer. She gardened and churched and PTAed and was good and clever and kind. If the bomb went off now, it would kill Callie Bristow.

I hurried to pass her and drew even with a chattering, ribald, eager group of boys, all bearded, all denimed, all very young and very alive.

"Shit, man, he's it! I mean nobody can match him, but nobody!"

"Okay, Bernie, okay. You got your ticket to Tel Aviv?"

I hurried again, then stumbled to a stop. The crowd had shifted and for an instant there was a clear space, a perfect view of the defense minister — and he was only thirty feet away.

I looked across that short, short space and for a moment our eyes met and held and I felt that quick electric thrill which would be any woman's response to him. Slim and tall, he stooped a little to listen courteously to a small birdlike woman, her fur turban sleek and shiny as a raven's feathers. His vigor, his maleness was accentuated by his silence, by his grave and serious face, his mocking and vibrant eyes that met mine, with a swift appraisal and a clear and unmistakable invitation.

A dangerous man, dangerous to peace and placidity and comfortable assumptions. Dangerous and beautiful, his eyes as black as the sea at night, his beaked nose predatory and commanding, his ruddy face the color of the desert sand at sunrise.

I tightened my hands on the package and looked, a swift, desperate, hunted look, at the fire exit, so far away, so effectively barricaded by students and professors and ladies from town. If I went that way, they would die. If I went straight ahead, a magnificent man and his ring of admirers would die.

"What's wrong, Janey? For God's sake, what's wrong?"

Julian towered over me. His great warm hands gripped my shoulders.

"Julian, oh Julian!" Then I tried to slip free from his grasp. "Get away from me, Julian. There's a bomb in this package and if he sees you talking to me he may explode it right now. Please, Julian."

For an instant Julian's eyes were as blank and unfathomable as the bleak granite of a Vermont peak, then his face, his wonderfully mobile face, broke up into a huge smile, he tossed his floppy mane of silver hair and chummily slipped one arm around my shoulders.

From a pace away, anyone would see that he was enjoying himself hugely, regaling a friend with a hilariously funny anecdote. But his soft quick words, reaching my ear alone, gave me hope.

"Where is he?"

"Near the door, Julian. Red hair and a beard and a navy blue coat. Do you see him?"

Julian laughed and his clear gray eyes swept the far side of the room. "All right, I see him. Now, quickly girl, who is he and why are you carrying a bomb? And how the hell can he blow it up from over there?"

All this and the smile never wavered on his face.

"They kidnapped Margaret. They are holding her and Willamae, my maid, at Willamae's mother's farm. They said they would let them go if I presented this package to the defense minister. But, Julian, I didn't know it was a bomb! Not until a boy almost knocked it out of my arms and I saw Morgan . . ."

"Morgan?" Julian asked sharply.

"The man with red hair. He jumped back when he thought the box was going to fall, jumped back and covered his face with his hands."

Julian was nodding and grinning and his right hand was slipping into his pants pocket. He drew out a pocketknife and pulled out a small, sharp blade.

I saw it and once again the ugly sensation of despair swept over me. "Julian, don't be a fool! You can't get to him with a pocketknife! And it wouldn't help anyway because he has this plastic case in his pocket, it looks like a transistor radio, and I'm sure that somehow he can signal and make the bomb explode!"

"It's a clever idea," Julian said generously. He moved until he was a little sideways to me. "Now look, Janey, you keep my hands out of view of the door and you nod and talk and laugh with me. Laugh and laugh. Your life depends on it."

With a broad smile and perfectly steady hands, he gently tipped the edge of the package up. For an impossibly long time, perhaps five seconds, he studied the package, looking at the bow, gingerly tracing the path of the ribbon along the sides and top of the box.

I could see the weave of the threads in that ribbon. I could count the uneven thicknesses in that silver band.

Julian ran one finger, lightly as the touch of a cat's whisker, around the rim of the box.

"Yes," he murmured, "it could be electronically rigged. Nothing shows in the ribbon. Of course, it might be triggered by lifting the lid. Well, we'll just have to see, won't we?" Then his companionable mutter sharpened. "Talk, Janey! Laugh!"

I tried to smile and through a rigidly widened mouth I told him where Willamae's mother's farm was. "Please, Julian, if you get out of this, get the police. Have them rescue Margaret and Willamae. They are unconscious. Drugged."

The tip of Julian's knife slid along the side of the box, loosening the sky-blue paper. Then, as quickly and deftly as a surgeon, he sliced the paper just above the bottom and just

168

below the lid and the paper fell away, revealing the innocuous-appearing white pebbled cardboard side of the box.

His fingers felt lightly and gently over this uncovered side. "This man and another? One more?"

"One, I think." I was watching his hand and it was hard to push words past the dryness in my throat. "I don't know who the other man is, Julian, but he's supposed to be watching us right now. Oh God, the defense minister is starting to walk toward the dais. Everyone will be sitting down."

"Can't hurry now," Julian muttered. He still smiled but sweat beaded his forehead and trickled down the sides of his face.

He paused for an instant, took a deep breath, then again the tip of his knife began to cut and he was slicing into the box.

I stood absolutely still. As though that would help! But the body has to respond as best it can. I didn't move. I didn't breathe. I didn't even watch the thinning crowd or notice that another admirer had intercepted the defense minister, keeping him from the speaker's table. Nothing mattered but the steadiness of Julian's long slender hand wielding the knife and the skill of his other hand as he peeled back the cardboard and, after a pause, reached inside the box.

# XIX

"God," he breathed softly. "I don't know, Janey. I may not be able to do it. It isn't triggered electrically. It's a plastic explosive and it's rigged to go off when the lid is lifted. If I can disengage the blasting cap, we'll be all right. Hold it steady, very steady."

A muscle flickered at the side of Julian's mouth. Gently, so gently, his hand pulled.

I closed my eyes.

"Infernal stuff," he said softly. Then a laugh bubbled in his voice. "You can open your eyes now, Janey."

I looked and in his hand he held a disc-shaped mass that looked like nothing so much as yellowed wax.

"Welcome back to the land of the living, Janey. We're all right now. I've defused it and, without a detonator, this yellow clump is harmless." He shook his head in relief. "It was enough plastic explosive to blow you and me and quite a few of our brethren wherever lost souls go." Then Julian frowned. "Your friend is starting this way."

I pushed the box into Julian's free hand. "Get the police, Julian!" I swirled around and started for the fire exit, swerving to avoid the scattered people who had yet to sit down. I hurried, ignoring Julian's call, "Janey! Janey!" and the surprised and curious faces turning toward me. I didn't look back or to either side. I only had eyes for that shiny, steel-colored exit door.

Everyone was beginning to look at me now. You cannot

run quietly in high heels.

"Janey, Janey, what's wrong?" Callie Bristow's voice.

I pushed through the heavy fire door and heard Callie call once more before the massive door swung shut, sealing away all noise except for the clatter of my shoes as I ran down the cement stairs. My side ached already and a sharp little pain jabbed down my right side, but I had to run, run to Margaret. I had to reach the farm first.

Down one flight, down another, and now I could hear someone on the stairs above me. Faster, faster I ran. At the base of the steps I rushed to the door and pushed through it out into the rain.

Frightened, fighting for breath, driven by past grief and future horror, yet I savored the stinging shock of the icy winter-chilled rain. I was alive. I had not, this past half hour, expected to feel again the exquisite agony of flesh chilled to the bone. I was cold and scared, frantic with anxiety, and at the same time more alive than I had ever been. I ran and my feet splashed through ankle-deep puddles. The rain, so thick it seemed like a sheet of water, plastered my dress against my body. But I ran like a free thing, like a fish effortlessly moving with a wave, like a glider soaring on the crest of the wind. I ran and felt as one with the wildness of the storm.

At the end of the Union I left the broad paved walk and ran up the slope that backed up to the administration building. I knew that just to the east of the building was a hedge-lined path that ran parallel to the Sinclair Street parking lot and was a far shorter route than the one Morgan and I had taken to the Union.

The thick well-tended lawn held under my feet. I ran and my luck ran with me. I passed the administration building and there, dark lines apart, I saw the twin shapes of the head-high hedges. Without breaking my pace, I turned into that gloomy avenue and fairly flew the long, lonely way. Fifty yards ahead, hanging in the storm-dark sky, nimbused in the rain, shone the first of the lamplights of the Sinclair Street parking lot.

Working through a break in the hedge, I was in the parking lot and there, across the mass of cars, parked on the grass, was the black Mercedes.

Lightning split the eastern sky and in the wavering greenish half-light I looked back toward the Union. The belltower jutted up black against the sky. The rain curved like a silver curtain in the bright, brief flash of lightning. Heavy black clouds blotted out the horizon until the sky seemed cupped just overhead, just out of reach. Trees bent beneath the wind and the last clinging leaves were wrenching free.

Nowhere in that greenish, half-seen landscape was there human movement. The trees, sloping grounds, and beleaguered buildings, rain pelting against them, belonged to the storm.

To the storm and to me. I ran on into the parking lot, passing one rank of cars, then another, and then a third, all dark and lifeless. I reached the Mercedes and I no longer felt the icy sag of my dress or the sharp prick of the rain. In a moment, in a breath of time, I would slide behind the wheel and be on my way to Margaret. In only a moment.

I knelt by the left front fender and put my hand up behind the metal panel that curved over the wheel.

I put my hand up so confidently. Where the arc of metal reached its apex, where the artfully mottled metal curved, there would be a smell magnetic box and within it an extra set of keys. My fingers pressed against the cold, mud-daubed curve of steel, pressed and felt and found nothing.

Slowly at first, then more quickly and, finally, frantically, my hand groped and probed all along the interior of the fender, tearing away great globs of sticky clay, tearing and pulling and finding only the unyielding steel.

They had to be there! They were always there. The extra set of keys. "Just in case," Paul had said when he bought the clever little magnetic holder. Just in case. Dear God, if ever I had need of keys, it was now. If ever all that mattered hung in the balance, it was now.

Once more, forcing my hand to move slowly, I felt along the arc of the fender, back and forth, up and down. "Please, please," I could hear myself crying and then, just as I despaired, my fingers found the case where it had slipped down almost to the rim of the fender.

I pulled it out and was opening the little metal box when I heard the hard slap of running feet. I half turned and raised my head high enough to see over the hood of the nearest car and there, spotlighted for an instant beneath a lamppost, was Morgan.

He was coming here and he would take the Mercedes from me. He would be here before I could unlock the door and get underway. Desperately I scrambled around on the ground beside the Mercedes. A rock, a stick, anything! But there were only soggy lumps of grass.

The hard slap of running feet changed pitch. He was on the blacktop now and the soft asphalt muted the sound.

I was backing away from the front of the car, backing on all fours, awkwardly but swiftly. I moved into the embrace of the weeping willow and the long wet branches hung around me.

Morgan would have to unlock the Mercedes. For that moment he would be vulnerable, and for that moment only. I grabbed at the trunk of the willow but it was much too thick and springy to be broken. For an instant my arm caught in a dangling, clinging branch. I wrapped my hand in a length of branch and pulled. That wouldn't work, either, but. . . .

Morgan, breathing hard, splashed through a deep puddle and ran heavily to the Mercedes. As he stood by the door and reached a hand into his pants pocket, I was pulling at my belt, the thick-woven cord that looped around my waist and knotted in front.

I tugged and the cord knotted tighter.

Morgan was pulling his hand out of his pocket.

I yanked savagely at the belt and the knot slipped free. I tore the cord from the belt loops, caught an end in either hand, stepped out of the entangling branches of the weeping willow, raised my hands, and moved silently toward Morgan.

He had the keys out now and was leaning forward, fumbling at the lock, his hands impatient.

Later I would wonder whether I hesitated, but at that moment I was beyond thought. I saw him only as a mortal threat to Margaret, my blood, my bone. I moved as quietly, as inexorably, as a gull slants through the sky at a fish glinting in the water.

Closer and closer and then I was upon him and the sodden cord flipped over his head and closed on his neck. He had a moment, an instant only, to begin to struggle, to make a violent, urgent noise in his throat. Then the line was taut and with my knee hard against his back, I yanked backward with all my strength.

The crack as his neck broke was startlingly loud and clear and distinct. It sounded like a snapped stick, but harsher. Then the vividness of the sound was lost as I tried to push away his limp and heavy body. He toppled back against me and I was falling, and we sprawled together on the muddy ground.

I pushed at him in an agony of horror, my hands slipping on the slick finish of his blue coat. I struggled to get free, to roll that unbelievably heavy weight away. It didn't really take long, it only seemed unending. I would never forget the pressure of his body, the unceasing wash of the rain against my straining face and the hollow thump when his head rolled against a tree root.

Finally I was free. I clambered to my feet and stumbled to the car. As I unlocked the door I realized that I still held the belt to my dress. The belt that. . . . I wanted to be sick, violently sick. Instead, I tossed the belt away from me onto the car seat, climbed in and began to think about what lay ahead.

How long had it been since I'd heard the swift slap of Morgan's running feet? Five minutes? Surely not more. It seemed a lifetime ago. For him, it was.

Was it possible that the man from Florence was already on his way to the farm? Could he reach the farm before me?

I was turning the key in the ignition when I realized that I would be powerless to defend Margaret even if I arrived first. The road, that narrow, graveled road, was no more than a half track. Once in, I would be trapped by any incoming car. Margaret and Willamae and Willamae's mother, if, please God, they still lived, would be groggy and sick, no help at all.

Quickly I jumped out of the car, ran to Morgan, and knelt by him. He lay face down, and already his body seemed a part of the earth, pressed there, dark and heavy and inert. I could not reach inside his coat where he lay. I began to try to turn him. The rain, that unceasing, icy rain, splashed against us and my wet hands found no purchase on that slick material. I was pushing my arm beneath him when the strident howl of a siren sounded. It was coming toward the campus. Desperately I tried again to turn him. The siren screamed nearer and nearer and then I saw the flashing red lights as the police car turned into the Sinclair lot. I dared not stay by Morgan's body. I was on my feet and running to the Mercedes.

I slammed into the front seat and started the car, and the

sweet purr of her motor steadied my nerves. She was in gear and bumping over the curb into the parking lot as the police car stopped at the Union service entrance.

Somehow I forced myself to drive at a calm pace, as if sharp, hard fear weren't eating at my soul. I even stopped at the exit and looked both ways. A thoughtful driver, a cautious driver.

A driver who would stop for no one, for nothing.

One block from the Union. Two. My foot began to press on the accelerator. Three blocks. Go, my God Janey, go. He may be ahead of you. Even now. And Margaret is lying on that bed, her thin face turned to one side, a flaccid pale cheek pressed against the pillow. Go, Janey, go.

The Mercedes clung to the rain-swept streets. Her wide, arced wipers slanted back and forth, back and forth, sweeping away the water, and her strong lights danced in the rain. Faster and faster I sped through the dark, storm-drenched afternoon, heavy black clouds diminishing the sky until the horizon seemed to crowd against the earth.

Three blocks more and I was wheeling up the access ramp and onto the crosstown expressway. The Mercedes barreled along the freeway, passing every car with precision and ease. The expressway emptied into the interstate and the speedometer needle crept up to eighty and stayed.

Three miles. Four, and then the road marker signaled Highway 87, two miles. The rain began to lessen. I drove faster, faster. The even, swishing beat of the wheels matched the pulse in my throat. I hurtled through the black afternoon, a part of a magnificent machine, as mindlessly driven as its cylinders, as suspended from my past as from my future, existing only to struggle for my own.

I slowed a little, very little, to careen off the interstate and onto Highway 87, then picked up that speed again immedi-

176

ately. This was a two-lane road, a good enough road on an ordinary day. But this was no ordinary day.

Ordinarily I would not pass on hills. Ordinarily I would not pass on curves. I passed a double-loaded trailer near the top of a hill and the angry blare of his horn followed me to the crest. The Mercedes topped the rise and in front of me, moving so slowly it scarcely seemed to move at all, was a rattletrap coupe. Somehow I swerved around it in time.

I passed every car and truck on the road before me and still the six miles seemed like sixty.

The road flowed with the curving hills, up and down. On either side the winter-bared trees thrust gray-brown branches up into the cloud-laden sky and the hills were as stark and dreary as an untended grave.

The Mercedes hissed along the wet highway and suddenly a new fear gripped me. Had I missed the turnoff? Could the marker have fallen since morning, the rain swirling around an unsteady pole, washing away the supporting earth?

For a moment I lessened the pressure on the accelerator and for the first time since I'd turned onto the highway, the Mercedes' speed slipped under eighty. Seventy-five. Seventy. Should I turn around? What had the odometer read when I'd turned onto Highway 87? I was supposed to go six miles east, then turn right onto State Highway 14. How far had I come?

It seemed a million more than six.

Then the road sign glittered in the beam of my headlights, SH 14, ½ mile.

Seventy-five. Eighty. Eighty-five. The Mercedes hurtled to the top of the hill and over and then, coming closer every second, I saw a tableau that for an instant puzzled me. Then I understood, and despair curled around my heart.

# XX

My headlights bore brighter every second on the shambles of the red and white barricade that obviously had barred access to SH 14 and threw into sharp relief the bulk of the police car askew in the ditch. The red light atop the car still swung in a circle, wheeling skyward, then tracing a brief path over the stony ground.

In the instant that I saw and understood, I realized too that it must have just happened. The door of the tip-tilted car was beginning to open up into the rain.

He was ahead of me. I knew it was him, the man from Florence. He had bulled his way though the barricade. And I knew why. Margaret had seen him. Willamae and her mother had seen him. And he knew he could count on me to rush to the farmhouse. And he was right. I had, of course, told Julian where the farm was. I could trust Julian to get the police. But that would take time and I could not wait. I had to reach Margaret before the man from Florence did.

Now I knew that I had not been fast enough. He was in front of me. The Mercedes had to slow a little to make the turn onto the blacktopped state highway, but only a little. I made that turn at fifty and heard the shouts and even caught the warning from the wrecked policemen, but I did not stop.

The beautiful black car skated her way down that slick blacktop and ahead, against the stormy sky, I saw the shine of headlights, a car speeding up a hill. I drove faster, so fast that

I felt the wheels must be skimming the asphalt, and faster. The margin between holding and leaving the road must have been measurable in millimeters.

So a bridge was out. That was what the policemen had shouted. But that would not save Margaret and Willamae. Or me. There was no bridge in the five miles before the weathered country store and the graveled road that led to the half track.

No natural barrier would save my daughter this afternoon. Nor could I hope for help from the police in time. The wrecked patrolmen at the barricade had radioed, angrily no doubt. Even now a patrol car was probably speeding toward SH 14. The patrolmen might even know they were dealing with something more serious than a broken barricade. They might know they were seeking a killer because Julian would have told the police by now. The patrolmen might know this and know that Willamae and Margaret were prisoners. A dozen cars might be streaming down the highway at this very moment, but none of them would be in time to save them.

The lights of the car ahead flickered up into the stormy sky again and I pushed the accelerator to the floor and held it there.

How far ahead was he?

The road swooped up and down and now I saw the gleam of his headlights just one hill ahead. I was gaining.

My hands gripped the wheel vise tight. My eyes strained to see through the rain. I poured every ounce of my will into my driving.

I topped another rise and my heart jumped and a tight smile of triumph broke the tension of my face. I saw clearly and unmistakably the gleam of his taillights. Then they were gone but I was closer, much closer, and I knew they would shine longer in my eyes when I reached the next crest. And they would be nearer.

Thoughts, pictures, and half-formulated schemes tumbled in my mind and mixed with the roar of the motor and the swishing whine of the tires.

A weapon. I had no weapon. I had nothing. Nothing but absolute determination.

The Mercedes rocketed down the slope and began to curve up another hill. Abruptly, I pushed in the headlight knob. I was getting close now and the longer it was before he knew he was followed, the better.

Of course he would see me when I wallowed down the half track after him. If I slowed. . . . No, no, I could do nothing for Margaret and Willamae if he had time to get out of his car and hurry across that forlorn, grassless plot and climb those rickety steps and. . . .

He must not reach them before me.

This time as I topped the hill I saw the whole shape of his car just reaching the next rise. It was a dark green Ford and he was having trouble with it. The right rear wheel wobbled. He was hitting the top speed he could make and still keep the car under control.

I could catch him. I was sure of it now. I hunched a little closer to the wheel and edged my beautiful car past eighty-five.

I watched the Ford careen around a curve, now only about a hundred yards ahead of me.

Time was running out, the feet and yards speeding past, the slick black asphalt slipping beneath the Mercedes and then I saw, perched on top of the hill like a tattered gray cat, the little country store. Red taillights winked through the rain as the Ford swung to its right on the country road.

When there is nothing to lose and everything to gain,

attack. When hesitation assures defeat, attack.

There was one possibility, one faint chance, but I must time it precisely, exactly.

The Mercedes reached the little store and turned — and began to slide. I swung the wheel to the left, turning into the slide, and she came around and steadied, but it had been a very near thing. My heart raced and I refused to think what might happen, what would surely happen, to Margaret and Willamae if the Mercedes slipped into a ditch now.

I drove a little more slowly. I held the wheel with my right hand and pressed the window button with my left. The window rolled down and the icy rain splashed inside. I drove and listened and for a long moment could not separate the noises, the silken rustle of the rain, the throaty murmur of the Mercedes, the creak and moan of the wind-whipped trees, the unfamiliar squashy sound of the wheels turning through muck. Then I heard it ahead of me, the straining whine of the Ford's motor.

The road snaked among trees. Only the strewn gravel made it possible for the cars to ride over the mud. It was clear that this road was a second-thought road, fashioned along lines of least resistance, giving pride of place to big trees, going around, not through.

I stayed just far enough behind that the driver of the Ford wouldn't see me, but close enough to hear the laboring whine of his car. It was a delicate balance.

I couldn't make my move until the very last moment as the Ford was pulling to a stop in that bleak, grassless patch of ground in front of the narrow farmhouse. The graveled road was too winding, too meandering for my plan. The half track, that narrow, pathlike trail to the farm, ran straight and true for its half mile. A half mile. That was enough.

The Mercedes curved to the right, around a clump of

maples, and again the twinkling of taillights marked the turning of the Ford, this time into the half track. Slowly, gingerly, like a leopard slithering onto an overhanging rock, the Mercedes crept up to the entrance to the half track.

I waited for a moment, then eased into the half track, my hand tight on the shift. Not yet, I knew, not quite yet.

My hands were hot on the steering wheel. A pulse throbbed in my throat. The taillights were out of sight now. My destroyer was moving ahead. Who was he? Andrew with his inviting eyes and sensuous mouth? The jaded novelist with the worn, used face? Alan James who looked so bland and self-satisfied in his photo?

Soon enough, I would know. And I would have my chance. My only chance.

I waited yet a moment more. It could only have been seconds that I waited but it was long enough to remember Margaret running through the leaves at the park. How long ago it seemed, and it was only yesterday. Monday. A Monday that began with the taillights of Paul's car disappearing in the early-morning grayness. That was Monday and this was Tuesday and what a difference it made. A little girl laughing in the park, reaching up to catch her mother's hand. Such a safe, cared-for, loved little girl.

I shifted into low and held back for an instant more. Paul, Paul, if I had known I would have run out of that class in California and never stopped beside your desk to talk. Oh, Paul, I am so sorry. I never meant to bring you grief. Paul's daughter with a narrow, grave face. Paul's daughter whom he loved so much.

I let out the clutch and pressed on the accelerator. The Mercedes picked up speed quickly, quickly, and she began to plunge down the half track, wild and free and utterly unstoppable.

The Mercedes burst out of the half track into that bleak plot of ground. It all happened so quickly that my memory of the house and ground and car telescoped into a jumble of images.

One image would always be clear and distinct in my mind.

In that brief span of time, as the Mercedes plummeted across the yard, I saw the dark green Ford, saw it stop, saw its brake lights flash on, and saw, for one unforgettable moment, a well-remembered face.

Andrew only realized his danger, felt the brush of death's wing, at the last instant. Perhaps he heard the steady roar of the Mercedes engine. He twisted around in his seat. His darkly handsome face flushed with anger. He raised his hand and I glimpsed the dark metal of a gun and then the Mercedes crashed into the back of the Ford with a horrendous, grinding, jolting impact, lifting up the Ford and throwing it forward against an oak tree, smashing the trunk forward as the tree jammed the hood backward.

The force of the impact wrenched my hands from the wheel and flung me hard against the leather dash. Breathless, aching, scarcely able to think, still I somehow managed to scramble up from the floorboard and back onto the seat, and then I saw the great whirling shape of the flames that enveloped the Ford, overwhelming it in a searing cascade of fire.

# XXI

The heat of the flames began to pop huge blisters on the crumpled front of the Mercedes. I could no longer even see the back of the green Ford. My skin ached from the intensity of the heat and it was so hot, even with the windshield between me and the flames, that it hurt to draw air into my lungs.

Frantically I tried to open the door. It was jammed.

The heat was worse now, worse every second.

I pulled myself over into the back seat and again yanked at the hot metal of a door handle. No matter how hard I pulled, the door would not open.

The yellow-red flames were licking the windshield now, flickering and curving a little higher and a little farther every instant.

Desperately I tried to roll down the window. Slowly, grudgingly, the window, warped in its frame, began to move. It was down an inch. Two. Five. The window was halfway down now and the flames were beginning to reach past the front window, almost to the back. It stuck three-fourths of the way down but I was clawing my way out, out into the blessedly cool air, heavy with misting rain.

I tumbled awkwardly onto the wet red clay but, even as I fell, I was trying to get to my feet. Where was he? Where was Andrew? He had a gun. I fell and was up in an instant.

The heat forced me back from the wreckage. Then I saw the green Ford fully for the first time. It was a ball of flame, surrounded, enveloped, enclosed by fire. Within that curving mass of flame, I saw a strangely shrunken, blackened mass that was Andrew.

I watched for a moment, then turned away and hurried toward the narrow, gray house.

I was loosening the clothesline that held Margaret and Willamae and her mother when the police helicopter landed. Above the policeman's calls, I heard Julian shout, "Janey, Janey! Are you here?"

"Julian, up the stairs, quickly. Oh, Julian, they are still unconscious!"

Everything happened in a blur then. Julian pulled himself up into the room and very gently helped transfer the three of them to the waiting arms of the ladder. We were all in the helicopter and to the hospital in less than twenty minutes. I held Margaret in my arms, my face pressed against hers, too fearful to cry, too intent upon her survival even to think of Morgan and Andrew and the fact that I had killed them and everything that that would mean.

It was evening before I wearily stepped out into the hall from Margaret's room at the hospital in answer to Julian's low-voiced call.

I reached out to touch his arm. "She's sleeping naturally now, Julian. She's going to be all right."

"Thank God, Janey. And there's more good news. Paul's on his way home. He should be here any minute now."

I swayed on my feet at that. Julian caught me up and helped me to a chair. "I'll get the doctor, Janey. We've none of us thought what you've been through!"

"No," I said sharply. "No." I held Julian's hand tightly. What was I going to say to Paul? How could I face him? To come home and find his wife a murderess, not once, not twice, but many times over when the story of the plane came out. The disgrace and ugliness of having his wife in jail.

I looked up at Julian. I could feel the tears sliding down my face. I hadn't even thought of what lay ahead!

"Don't cry, Janey," Julian urged. "I'll see to everything. You don't even need to talk to the police tonight. The lieutenant said it could wait until you felt up to it." Julian squeezed my hands in his own huge ones. "It's really incredible how brave you have been. Chasing out to the farm alone, unarmed, and then having the courage to ram right into the back of Channing's car. We saw it from the helicopter. Thank God you were able to get out of the Mercedes before it burned, too. Well, it was your turn for a little luck."

I forced myself then to ask, "Julian, about Morgan, have the police . . ." and I couldn't finish. I dropped my face into my hands.

"Oh, Janey, I'm so sorry!" Julian said quickly. "No one's told you! Please, you don't need to be frightened. He'll never bother you again."

Wonderingly, I raised my face to look at Julian.

He frowned, then asked hesitantly, "Janey, do you think you can bear up to one more shock?"

I nodded uncertainly.

"The police have decided that Channing went berserk. He strangled Morgan in the Sinclair Street parking lot."

I must have looked astounded because Julian said quickly, "Yes, it's true. The police haven't unearthed the whole picture yet and they may never know all of it, but they think the two of them were killers hired by the Black September movement to liquidate the defense minister. And it was just your bad luck that they decided you would be a natural to hand the bomb to Levin."

"I see," I said slowly.

He grabbed up my hands again. "I know it's all a shock and it's been a frightful experience, but you can relax now,

186

Janey. Paul will be here soon and everything will be all right."

Yes, everything would be right. I was safe now, but more than that, I was free from the past, free for all time, free to glory and grow in true love, the love that builds instead of destroying.

I heard those familiar, quick solid steps before Julian did and I jumped up and turned to run, my arms open wide.

"Oh, Paul, I'm so glad you've come."